I0762167

The Cornerstones of Happiness

The Cornerstones Of Happiness

Jeremy Taylor

ANDEAN PUBLISHING
NEW YORK CITY
2020

Andean Publishing
1420 York Avenue
New York, NY 10021

Taylor, Jeremy // The Cornerstones of Happiness
Jeremy, Taylor // Andean Publishing

Library of Congress Control Number: 2020918025
ISBN 9781736127735

TO ANDREA

LOVE MUFFIN, YOU'RE
MY CORNERSTONE
OF HAPPINESS

Nothing is more exhausting than endlessly working on "yourself." When you offer your whole Being fully to Love, self-acceptance arises spontaneously. May I rest in our Oneness, dear Divine!

—TOSHA SILVER

Contents

The Cornerstones of Happiness

Prologue

A problem cannot be solved by the same level of consciousness that created it.

—ALBERT EINSTEIN

A girlfriend of mine once said, "I'm so sick with the flu, it feels like I was hit by a truck."

Let's say she was hit by an actual Mack truck. You visit her at the hospital, point to her broken bones, damaged limbs, and misshapen face, and what do you say? You say, "Wouldn't having the flu right now be *much* better, Coco?" (By the way, I used to be a stripper, so you may hear a lot of names like *Coco, Cookie, Chyna, Kitty, Aspen, Cinnamon,* and *Chardonnay.*)

Anyway, that's how I felt that day—like I was coming down with the flu. To a doctor, I'd appear normal, but what is "normal," exactly? And what kind of a doctor are we even talking about it? Is he a shrink? Is he cute?

What I mean is, everything was fine with me on the outside. Yet on the inside, I felt like my life was spiraling out of control into an entirely new dimension of despair. Some people believe mental disorders, including depression, are not real. Well, screw you for thinking that.

Wow, her attitude, you think. Maybe before we continue—just for fun—you should jump up and down on a stripper pole while a dirty man holds a dirty dollar bill in his dirty hand and you smile like it's your paycheck.

Any more questions about attitude?

What could possibly go wrong with a robot (or at least I felt like a robot) of the twentieth century, you ask? Haven't we advanced so far beyond the realm of reality? We've landed on the moon, cured AIDS (OK, not quite), and learned to deliver packages in two days.

Well, here's what was wrong with me: The formula for happiness—yes, it's a thing, a whole formula—that I'd meticulously crafted was collapsing on me after years of painstaking research and undeniable evidence, while I stood under the crumbling building without a hard hat, soon to be buried in my own mistakes.

I'll get back to that vision in a second. First, allow me to introduce myself as if we're in sixth grade. (I frequently feel trapped there, in my memories, when I'm young, stupid, and naive. My girlfriends and I are giggling and gossiping over extensive phone calls that last way past midnight.) Do you remember those happy times?

We used to fill in each other's diaries and answer quizzes, like "Name, Hobbies, Pet Peeves." Here's mine from the actual sixth grade, uncovered from a memorabilia pile:

Name: Lindsay North.

Nickname: Fanta.

Age: thirteen. But if my boyfriend asks, I'm eleven.

Favorite color: hot pink.

Where were you born? Orlando, Florida.

My hobby: dancing.

I'd hate it if I got: fat.

My life goal: to find happiness.

Nothing had changed, evidently, except for my age, nickname, and hobbies.

I'm now twenty-six, but if a boyfriend asks, I'm twenty-two, and my nickname is Chardonnay because that's what I used to drink at Cookie's strip club. (Yes, the owner's name was Cookie, and she named the club after herself.)

My hobbies are running, dieting (also called *starving*), and reading self-help books (which is barely a hobby, more an obsession). That last one intertwines with my sixth-grade life goal of finding happiness, which then meant finding my mother.

What do I mean by finding my mother? Meet "safe-haven law." The Florida statute says that mothers are allowed to abandon their babies at a fire station, hospital, or ambulance—anonymously, if needed—without fear of prosecution. That's right, my friends; they can. The infant must be three days old or younger, and the biological parents have thirty days to change their minds. If you think that's cuckoo, don't hold your breath. The word *cuckoo* barely scrapes the surface of what went on in the upcoming years after Mommy dearest had abandoned me.

In general, if you read the news on your phone and notice an article that starts with "Florida Man" or "Florida Woman," please, avoid clicking the link. Usually, such articles are followed by "Pooped on Car from Streetlight" or "Arrested after Leaving Boyfriend to Die in Suitcase."

Anyway, as a Florida child, becoming bad mannered was barely a choice, considering my history. My foster parents tried their best, but if there's no will, there's no way. From an early age, I learned to look after myself—and if things went awry, to leave. That's what Mother did (so in a way, it's mom approved). If things go wrong, abandon.

Abandoning had become my forte: jobs, relationships, and friendships. I've flown all over the country searching for answers, the meaning of life.

At my latest job, I was a live-in nanny, and isn't it ironic that, perhaps unconsciously, I'd chosen to work at a place where there was a mom? At the strip club, too, there was what we called a house "mom"—Cookie, who took care of us, paid us, and provided advice. It's obviously no coincidence, either, that I seek out older female figures in my life, be they friends or employers, all because of my unquenchable thirst for a mother. Or at least that's what I learned from self-help books. "Look deep inside yourself. Explore where your insecurities stem from. Love yourself." And similar crap.

After a decade, I'm done analyzing myself. Well, analyze this for yourself all you wish: In the past eight years alone, I acquired a deck of ex-boyfriends, made a hundred meaningless friendships, and worked at a dozen places. I've been a waitress, a stripper, and a live-in nanny—all seemingly unrelated jobs but with one thing in common: all jobs paid cash.

What's so important about cash, you ask?

First of all, I'm indisputably (head over heels) in love with cash. I love holding and counting dollar bills. If they're in my hands, I know for a fact they're mine. Nothing was ever mine growing up. I've never owned a house, and with my nonexistent credit, nobody would trust me with a lease. I've never even owned a pet. But this I know for sure: if I am holding cash, it's always mine.

Why cash, especially when a growing number of people hate it? I've learned to distrust credit cards—that simple. Overhearing a stressed foster father continuously lash out at his wife because of his gambling debts stays deep under your skin. Plus, I'm an independent, wandering soul, and owing anyone is the opposite of that. That's who my mommy was, too, in a sense. An independent soul. Perhaps she was in a financial struggle (which is neither here nor there). You don't wait for nine months to leave your child behind, and if you must or are out of choices, abortion is legit on the table. Not to say I wish I were dead. My story is more nuanced than that.

Eventually, most of my stripper girlfriends moved on from the craft, put themselves through college, or gave birth. I tried an associate degree but was too distracted and was often swept away by romance. (Speaking of giving birth, it's alleged that the pain equivalent of giving birth is like being kicked in the nuts. Nobody can check the authenticity of such a statement because a man can't give birth, and a woman can't be kicked in the nuts. Let me put this into perspective, people. Coco gave birth to three kids, and yet no man I know wants to be kicked in the nuts twice. Well, I guess some do, but we'll get to that later.)

Do the math.

Last year, while going through a quarter-life crisis, I attempted to pinpoint where my unhappiness had set roots. I often wondered why I was different from other people because the women around me seemed happier overall. Was I unmotivated or less fortunate? Was it because I'd been abandoned at the hospital by Mother? Or was my problem related to a chemical imbalance in my brain? In which case, was there any hope at all?

I was desperately searching for answers because I was quickly losing faith and a desire to live. It definitely sounds dramatic. You know how the mind can overreact, right? Well, you don't know you're overreacting until much later—when it's too late.

I simply wished to disappear. Disappear to a land where there were no boyfriends, mothers, or self-hatred. I inhaled self-help books about relationships, self-sabotage, and parents—one bestseller after another. Wherever happiness was concerned, advice appeared similar. I highlighted passages like a mad scientist, paraphrasing authors' ideas. In fact, I discovered a formula for happiness, and it boiled down to four bullet points.

The cornerstones of happiness are as follows:

1. **A healthy body makes a healthy mind**. What you put in your body will affect you 100 percent. That includes spirituality and believing life is not just your ego. Which brings us to the second point.

2. **Be a part of your community and give back**. Volunteer. Since the dawn of time, humans have been social creatures, and together, we stood rigid against the enemy and natural disasters. Each person has her own unique way of connecting to the world through her craft or that special gift—talent. Which brings us to the third point.

3. **Vocation is not just money**. You were given a beautiful body and soul. You're now a part of your community. It's time to find and strengthen your natural abilities. If you find a craft you were born to do, you'll shine brighter

than any diamond. You'll fall in love with life and with your beautiful self. Which brings us to the last point.

4. **Once you fall in love with yourself—dearly and deeply—the right partner will materialize**. He'll fall in love with you for who you truly are: slim or fat, black or white, educated or not. With the right partner, you don't pretend to be better. You're honest. You're finally happy.

That sounds too simple to be true.

Part One

Astoria

Stop a moment, cease your work, look around you.

—LEO TOLSTOY

One

While at times, self-help books can sound like a bunch of religious hoopla, other times, they become oxygen and water, two elements needed for your survival. The four cornerstones of happiness could be misinterpreted as a cult mantra. Since I wasn't religious and was afraid of cults, I realized I could take these four points and apply them through my own, nonreligious filter.

Healthy body
Community
Vocation
Partner

Out of the four cornerstones, however, I had zero.

And indeed, I felt empty inside. Everywhere you looked, it was happiness this, happiness that—propaganda aimed at young, desperate women like myself who tried to become somebody in life. But how can you become someone without a solid foundation?

When you erect a building and want it to stand firmly on the ground, you need a stone at each corner: the cornerstones.

Can building a solid foundation for happiness be any different?

Are the four bullet points the pathway to happiness?

Is happiness nothing but a simple mathematical equation?

If happiness relied on the four cornerstones, I reasoned, then I'd apply them to my life. When considering "we are what we eat," I was just that: trash. I lied to myself and my friends about eating healthily, while in the privacy of my own bedroom, it was all about unhealthy chicken nuggets (and barfing to stay skinny). I admit, I'd been totally brainwashed by society's unrealistic standards for women. People regularly rip on supermodels for bulimia, anorexia, or orthorexia, but the models shouldn't be blamed. (If body-shaming decreased, eating disorders would too.)

When considering giving back and being a part of the community (through volunteering, for example), I had nothing to say.

The third cornerstone implies that finding a vocation that matters is essential, and again, I was at a loss. I worked as a live-in nanny, and my so-called vocation was insignificant, if not plain stupid. It was simply about cash, and I'll repeat: I love cash. Perhaps, though, self-help books had a point, I thought, and I should seek a meaningful vocation. The formula suggests that once we find a meaningful career, we'll fall madly in love with ourselves.

Last, the formula mentions relationships. A partner will love you once you love yourself.

It was self-explanatory, then, why I was single, unhappy, and hopeless. So before it was too late, I had to somehow climb out of the grave I was digging for myself.

Two

It was time to follow my own advice and apply the cornerstones of happiness to my life.

First, since I'd been an avid runner for two years, exercise was step one to have a healthier body. My diet of greasy foods had to change, and the barfing stopped. I started conducting so much research about nutrition, I could become a nutritionist. Turns out, there *are* ways to stay in shape by swallowing food! I took various multivitamins, made green smoothies with leafy vegetables, and avoided carbs. Eating organic had become second nature, especially since the food was free (perks of a live-in nanny and all). I felt stronger and more efficacious, and my weight never faltered. To sum up, the first cornerstone was under way.

I asked my girlfriends what my second cornerstone—helping others—could be, and my transgender friend Candace suggested I help her find a surgeon for the sex-reassignment surgery. She was transitioning to becoming a woman, which was a long and slow process already, but as a lawyer for a nonprofit dealing with transgender people and domestic violence, Candace barely had time to spend on herself.

She'd call and ask for updates and somehow bring up vaginas. Vagina this, vagina that. She was obsessed with getting a vagina. On top of her eighty hours of law work, she spent two hours weekly getting the required psychological evaluations prior to the surgery. Without a shrink's approval and written permission, the surgery was a no-go. But according to the shrink, Candace was unprepared, psychologically, to have her penis removed. She needed a shrink to tell her that? *Anyone* could tell her she was unprepared. First of all, Candace doesn't realize how uncomfortable it is to talk about vaginas. And second of all, there's more to being a woman than sexual organs. Women have class and poise, and two words we don't bring up in a conversation: *moist* and *vagina*.

One time, she called me and asked, "Does a vagina smell like fish if you don't wash it for two days?"

"Do you want to become a woman, Candace? Stop asking questions about smelly vaginas."

"But I want to learn. You're so lucky to have a natural, moist clit!"

"I never thought of myself as lucky. Just basic."

"Linds, be grateful for your peach. I would kill an endangered whale if that would have my penis cut off. But that stupid Dr. Stern wouldn't sign my papers. Still! After all the work! She says most people need five years of evaluations—at least. I can't wait any longer. It's been a year for me already."

"Then perhaps your shrink is right," I said.

"I work with hundreds of people, and they got their vaginas if they wanted one. Why can't I? I'll never be happy until I have a vagina!"

I doubted I could help Candace as a means to help myself, and I needed a plan B to get involved in my community. I started stealing food from my employer's fridge and donating it to the church across the street. I didn't really feel any different, and if anything, I felt more like a criminal, which wasn't helping me in any way. Robin Hood I wasn't, I realized. For the moment, I decided to leave the second cornerstone alone because maybe—just perhaps—the second cornerstone was something absolutely different.

When it came to the third cornerstone, vocation, many changes and improvements would be made. Without giving the Brownsteins two weeks' notice, I quit the nanny job. I didn't leave the parents high and dry, though—otherwise, I'd sound like a total "see you next Tuesday." Before quitting, I'd contacted Kitty, a former dancer from Cookie's strip club, who was job hunting, according to her Facebook posts. Whereas I wanted to find something "meaningful" and take my time searching, Kitty was desperate—two kids of her own, plus a sick mother. Out of desperation, the Brownsteins offered Kitty the position without checking her references. I planned on relying on money I'd managed to save up ($25,000) to act as a cushion while I looked for a meaningful vocation. The opposite of desperate. Easy, breezy, in fact.

By the way, Kitty was more of an acquittance, but we occasionally interacted on social media, liking each other's posts. She could totally have been a serial killer (after all, she had a killer smile and killer legs), but it wasn't my problem to deal with if the Brownsteins turned up dead.

I hadn't realized the nanny job was a hot Senate seat. My friend Chloe wanted to claw my eyes out for not offering it to her first. Chloe is one of those strange, cat-loving friends you have and whom you can only take in small, infrequent doses. I met her through Candace at a benefit for transgender people, and Chloe instantly became a frenemy. She made backhanded remarks about my weight (how undernourished I looked) or how my hair would be too frizzy one day. Her frequent complaints about everything made me keep her at arm's length.

She complained about not having a job but was picky about it, only applying for jobs she didn't qualify for. To sabotage herself, in my opinion. I thought Chloe didn't want a job per se; she sat on a huge inheritance and insurance money from her father's death, but she needed a reason to complain somehow. That's just who she was—a complainer. Perhaps, in the back of her mind, she thought that was her job in society—to complain.

Why work with all her money? I'd go and travel the world. But that's all she was obsessed with—finding a job to have something of her own, a pride thing, which I totally understand. To occupy her time, Chloe smoked weed and volunteered at soup kitchens for homeless people. To be honest, she started resembling the homeless more and more herself with her outfit choices.

Chloe called me as soon as she found out about Kitty.

"I have babysitting experience from way back," she said. "Do you know how many babies I feed soup at the shelter? And you didn't even think of *contacting* me, Lindsay? Who is that stupid Kitty, anyway?"

"Kitty is a long-time friend," I lied. "And she's not stupid. Kitty has been hired. End of story."

"It's called discrimination."

"Welcome to the club—where all of us are discriminated against. I keep asking myself the same question ever since my mom abandoned me."

"You always talk about your stupid mom!"

"And you always talk about wanting a job, Chloe, but you do nothing about it."

She hung up.

Having saved $25,000 in cash, I was comfortable being unemployed. I understood it'd take time before I found something meaningful, and in the meantime, I needed a cheap place to live. I looked in Astoria, Queens, where I lived five years prior while working at Cookie's strip club.

Within two days, I managed to find a small room in a four-bedroom walk-up for $600 a month. The two women who interviewed me, Lisa and Lise (which is also pronounced *Lisa*), my eventual roommates, were older than I was. From personal experience, they recognized what I was trying to accomplish with my life. You could say we clicked right away. We would share one bathroom, but they assured me it would work out fine with everyone's schedules.

The fourth roommate introduced himself to me like this: "Hi, I'm Liam, and I'm as gay as the day is long."

I'd never had gay or male friends before—straight men would rather discuss your breasts (not feelings), and gay men weren't a category of men I typically found in strip clubs in the past—but now I did! If I'd kept my thousands of goals written out, this is how it would look:

☑ Goal 11,102: Make a male friend.

☑ Goal 11,103: Make a gay friend.

Finding a legitimate job in New York City was stressful. I had no degree or experience for a position in a respectable field. To be honest, I had only a vague idea of what vocation could bring me happiness or if I had a calling. For instance, as a stripper, I made $300 per night—on a slow night. Two nights of work, and my rent was paid. But I gathered I wouldn't be young forever, and trust me when I say this: that industry heavily relies on hot girls in their prime, ages eighteen to twenty-three. That's also the age when the girls are the feistiest, which means most competitive, which means they bring big bucks to their clubs. At twenty-six, I was no longer prime or choice or even grade A beef. I was the manager's special—brown and untouchable.

Being a nanny is similar, in the sense that parents want to hire someone young and active. I loved babysitting at sixteen, when it was noncommittal. I'd watch neighborhood kids to earn money for movies, clothes, and cigarettes (when I used to smoke). At twenty-six, I no longer could fathom myself doing it. Again, back to the third cornerstone: If you don't love your job, you won't love your life. Plus, I had enough savings to start a career from scratch, even if that meant minimum wage and a long road climbing the corporate ladder.

To my absolute disgust, I got my very first credit card. My friend Nikita insisted I start building my credit, which she said would indirectly affect all four cornerstones of happiness. And she was right. When a message on the screen popped up with "You're approved!" my hands were shaking. I was *approved*. Ever since Mother had abandoned me, I never felt deserving of being approved. It was addicting. I applied for two more, and both were approved. Since I had somehow avoided using drugs, applying for credit cards became the alternative. Nikita said I had to charge often; otherwise, my credit score would stay at a constant.

Nikita is one of those friends who posts positive affirmations and cute animal videos on Facebook. I met her at

Sandy Hook Beach two years ago, an optimistic blonde Libra from New Jersey whose positive energy magnetized me—plus, drinks were involved.

Nothing seems to bother Nikita. Despite splitting her time as a nurse and running a small café in downtown Jersey City (her mom's legacy), three years prior, she fell in love with an employee of hers, Jesus, an illegal immigrant from Mexico who worked for her as a waiter. Their marriage lasted three years, and when we met, they were on the second. However, when Jesus received his citizenship last year, he divorced her without so much as giving her two weeks' notice. Adios. Like that. Thankfully, a prenup was in place, or I fear he would've taken her business. When I heard the news, I thought she'd be devastated; Nikita barely wavered, however. Like a total psycho. She kept on posting positive affirmations and cute animal videos as if nothing horrendous had happened. Now she's dating another illegal immigrant, Joaquin, a tall Chilean man five years younger—a waiter from her café—and they are getting married in September.

"You're not worried?" I asked her over the phone.

"About what?"

"What if all he wants is a green card, like Jesus?"

"You can't assume the worst. Look at the bright side—we'll have a prenup, *and* he's hot."

"That's the bright side?"

"So what's it to anyone if he wants a green card? I hear they're hard to come by. I'll find somebody else if I need to, and in the meantime, I'll have a hot husband who will be my baby daddy. This is the year when I'm getting pregnant. The clock is ticking."

"Do you wanna hang out?" I asked her.

"I can't. So much work."

"When did we become so busy that we can't hang out?"

"Life, you know?"

I took her refusals to hang out personally because I felt undeserving of her friendship. Being abandoned as a child had engraved insecurity in me, and that alone was a lifetime worth of self-improvements. I couldn't understand Nikita's free-balling attitude about her second marriage. How could she not see she was falling back into her old patterns?

In the meantime, I kept consuming self-help books, desperately trying to find *anything* about happiness.

There are so many ideas.

For example, in a book called *The Four Agreements*, the author argues that joy will come when you stop making assumptions, stop taking things personally, always do your best, and pretty much stop gossiping. In another self-help book, an author (whose name escapes me) quits her practice and goes to the Amazon in Brazil, seeking happiness in nature. (It works for her.)

Then I stumbled upon Confucius's ideas of happiness. He believed we are creatures of habit and often are stuck in our ruts. We behave according to how we grew up, repeating patterns of hatred and happiness. As a society, we're told to love ourselves as is and say, "Can't do anything about myself. I am who I am." But Confucius thought otherwise. He thought we must behave differently in different situations. That we should treat people differently based on their situation, no "all size fits all." Learning how to behave differently with different people and creating ritual spaces would make us happier. Trying to cater to everyone sounded absolutely insane and counterintuitive to everything I'd learned about happiness.

My own formula for happiness underwent a structural change, a transformation, an evolution of sorts. Being healthy was clearly crucial—my skin tone had improved, and my muscles had become tighter—but helping the community, for some reason, felt like a fraud. So I crossed volunteering off my list.

An important vocation and a meaningful relationship also remained unproven, two unreachable goals.

In the meantime, I loved living independently and realized that the second cornerstone of happiness was independence.

To sum up, the cornerstones of happiness changed:

Healthy body
Independence
Important vocation
Meaningful relationship

Three

I took my sweet time searching for a vocation, thinking that this time, I had to get it right. True, you can start working anywhere, with the attitude of "I can always quit," but the truth is, you won't quit. You've wasted all your energy on searching and interviewing, so you stay for a year out of courtesy, and the next thing you know, you're at a job as a nanny, and you hate it.

I multitasked between job searching and boyfriend searching, switching from one app to the other. It sounds like I didn't care whether I'd find a job. The truth is, I'd been surviving on my own since fifteen, and if I learned nothing else, I learned how to make a quick buck. So right then, I wasn't thinking of myself as lazy. I felt I deserved this impromptu mini-vacation before diving back into the professional world. Plus, chatting with guys helped me overcome boredom and elevated my low self-esteem.

My leisurely days were spent the following way. In the morning, I went running, which was the best way to get reacquainted with the neighborhood with which I'd lost touch. Five years earlier, things had looked different. I jogged daily, noting new restaurants, laundromats, and newly opened strip clubs. (The club where I worked five years ago had closed, and the neon COOKIE'S sign had been removed.) In the evening, I'd go for a cocktail with Chloe, Candace, or Kitty somewhere in Manhattan. And in between, I'd sandwich some time to bond with my roommates if they were available. Chloe constantly reminded me about the nanny job, whereas Candace only discussed vaginas, making me want to see both friends less. Kitty, a black girl, often brought up my white privilege, and while I never denied it, I preferred to avoid discussions about it so as not to further fuel animosity between us. I hated getting accused left and right, but the three of them were my only friends. Nikita was too busy posting aspirations and animal videos, it seemed, so I never saw her.

Four

The four-bedroom apartment where I lived was on the second floor, with one bathroom; a vast, galley-style kitchen with black and white tiles; and wood floors. Lisa and Lise had rented the place together four years ago and had been renting the other two bedrooms out. Liam moved in a year prior, and a tenant before me was another girl who'd moved away to California to pursue a career in filmmaking.

"More like whore-making for her," the judgmental Lisa said. As a joke, I assumed.

My bedroom was the smallest in size, and I could only imagine how much the three of them paid for their share of the rent. It was inappropriate to ask. Apartments in New York are notoriously overpriced, and you pay dearly for convenience, opportunities, and aspirations, sacrificing lots in the process. It seemed that Lisa and Lise cared none for matching dishes and received various plates from friends and family for free, even if some of them were chipped. Mason jars had become drinking glasses for water and wine. There were mugs with and without handles. Spoons and forks were from all sorts of periods, all mismatched, some antique and some modern. Liam ordered in a lot, so hundreds of food menus sat in a stack on top of the fridge. Thousands of plastic cutlery sets with individual packets of mayo, ketchup, mustard, soy sauce, duck sauce, salt, and pepper served as our condiments; no bottled condiments were found in the fridge.

Lisa and Lise appeared frugal by never ordering in, and if they did, they picked up their food to avoid delivery fees. I never understood why they worked so hard without spending a dime. We went through a roll of toilet paper per day, but neither of the girls ever purchased any—leaving it up to Liam or me. Same with paper towels. They rented books from the library and cooked everything themselves, be it snacks like dehydrated papaya, self-made celery juices, and even homemade roasted nuts. I'd never met a single New Yorker who cooked, and now I lived with two of them.

Lisa, who was taller than the three of us by a foot, worked from home as an accountant. This is why she said, without missing a beat, when I told her I opened two credit cards, "Don't spend more than you have, roomie." At thirty-seven, she was the oldest and took care of everything: cleaning, washing dishes, and taking down the trash. As a contractor to various firms and LLCs, Lisa managed people's assets remotely, and she'd set up her office in the living room by the window. Her ancestry was as complicated and nuanced as her personality. Her great-great-grandfather immigrated from Warsaw and married an American woman. Then their only child married someone from Germany, and their child married an American. After all the knots, Lisa was finally born in Delaware, a state she despised.

Her hair was jet black with some natural gray combed through, and the effect was stunning; her presence in a room added an instant grown-up factor, and I admired her sophistication and savoir faire. She was a total Scorpio: analytical, assertive, and resourceful. She could fix up a tasty meal out of Liam's leftovers, unwilling to spend money unless her choices ran out. She told me dry beans cost ninety-nine cents per pound, or a week of meals. Beans are unoriginal and bring flatulence (to Lisa), but when the price is right … Unlike Lisa, I'd never cooked anything but ramen and wasn't going to start anytime soon.

The second roommate, Lise, was such a Virgo, it was crazy—a kind and reliable overthinker. Her chubbiness or height never seemed to bother her, but her thick, wavy black hair, which we found all over the apartment, bothered everyone. She was born in New Jersey, but her family is originally from Ecuador, so she often spoke on the phone with her mom or clients in Spanish. She was thirty-five years old and a realtor. Half the time, akin to Lisa, she worked from home, doing "house research," which meant watching cat videos online on her computer. When Lise had a showing, she'd quickly doll up and leave for several hours somewhere in Astoria, never missing a scarf on her neck. Lise had been my realtor when I needed a room, and she'd accomplished two things: received a handsome commission and a roommate at once. The two of us instantly clicked, chatting as if we'd known each other for years. Like me, Lise was slightly disorganized and left her scarves all over the place the way I left my heels, but unlike me, a perpetual Aries, Lise was not in denial about it and made fun of herself. Her bedroom, like mine, was also a messy disaster.

Meanwhile, Lisa walked around like a mother after a toddler, picking up things after the two of us. Unlike Lisa, with her cold, analyzing demeanor, Lise became your best friend from the first encounter, and it was impossible to get angry with her. Several times now, Lise had used up my kale, believing it was hers, but I hadn't brought it up, thinking it'd make her upset. I figured I'd just eat hers someday. Lise had a boyfriend and spent lots of time at his place, but I'd never met him, Sammy. He looked cute in pictures, big biceps and white teeth. Teeth were quite literally all Lise cared about after her previous relationship.

Liam was a typical pleasure-seeking, overemotional Pisces, and he cried—more like wailed—a lot. He worked as a waiter at a Mexican restaurant down the street. Liam was thirty-two but looked maximum twenty-five, with perfect tan skin and a body to die for. As a creative sign, his anxiety fueled his art, and he carried a small sketch pad with him like a security blanket. His anxiety also fueled heavy drinking and weight lifting. What I'm trying to say is, Liam was crazy and unpredictable, your perfect textbook Pisces.

"Wait," I interrupted him, "weight lifting is what helps your anxiety?"

"Well," he said, "there's a shower at my gym where I find numerous hookups, which is why I must stay in tip-top shape."

"Why?"

"In the gay community, it's all about no fats, no femmes, no Asians. Welcome to the gay world, with all its body shaming."

"Yes," I said, "the gay world. Also known as *the* world."

Liam had thinning blond hair, which he wore slicked back or under a huge straw hat. He was an oxymoron. First, he claimed the sun damaged the skin, saying we must lather ourselves in sunscreen and wear protective clothing and sunglasses. Then he'd spend a week on Fire Island on a nude beach without wearing a thread. I just shrugged my shoulders.

Liam introduced me to a drag-queen show called *RuPaul's Drag Race*. I fell in love right away when RuPaul said, "If you can't love yourself, how in the hell can you love somebody else? Can I get an amen up in here?"

"Amen," drag queens shouted back.

At the end of each episode, RuPaul repeated the same sentence, and one evening, his message finally reached me. First, you must unapologetically fall in love with yourself, and then other people will fall in love with you as well—just like in the formula for happiness. If you're unhappy … how in the hell can you make another human happy?

That was the fourth cornerstone of happiness, according to self-help books. *Feel compassion for yourself*, they taught. *Love and comfort the inner child*. I'd been doing so much healing work and yoga and knew those thoughts were working. Slowly but surely. *Be kind and patient and blah, blah, blah*.

Lisa and I bonded on the fact that we lived in Singlesville and both used dating apps. If I purchased some wine for the two of us, we'd remain on the couch and share our potential matches with each other; her taste for men was all over the spectrum, whereas mine stayed constant. (When it came to wine, the stingy Lisa never returned the favor. I tried not to get disappointed, though, per my newly found practice of kindness and patience and blah, blah, blah.)

Five

After moving to Queens on May first, I'd gone on two dates, and both were complete disasters. See for yourself. The first guy was tall, dark, and handsome, but he ended up being a kleptomaniac. When the check arrived, he stole a candle, the food menu, and an empty beer glass from the next table. I was surprised he hadn't stuck me with the bill. The second guy was also tall, dark, and handsome, but somehow, we discussed his ex-girlfriend and how all women were gold diggers.

Lisa had no luck finding anyone either. The fourth cornerstone seemed out of reach for us, and I wondered whether it was a universal problem or if there was something wrong with us. (Self-help books insist it's always them and not *you*, but I wouldn't bet on it.)

Lisa and I had become best friends by bonding because of our failures. However convenient, though, apps are apps, and as I learned from self-help books, we're always under the impression that someone better will come along—you just have to keep looking. In this FOMO-driven society, we've stopped giving each other the time of day. One little imperfection, and there we go, writing them off because they failed to meet our insane criteria.

Check all that apply:

☑ Tall, dark, handsome.

☑ Rich, independent, altruistic.

☑ Pet-friendly, sense of humor, nonsmoker.

One wrong answer, and we're moving on. I added two more boxes to my list:

☑ No kleptomaniacs.

☑ No misogynists.

These days, we summarize our thoughts in tweets rather than writing full-on passages, and I received not-dissimilar messages on the apps. The conversation I'm about to share happened after the two failed dates. The guy wasn't really my type, chunky and awkward, but I'd been lowering the bar, thinking I should give him a chance.

"Hi, Lindsay, you're beautiful! My name is Matt. Let's chat."

"Thank you."

"No problem. How's it going?"

"I'm good, thanks. Applying for jobs. How about you?"

"Cool."

Two minutes went by, then seven, then fifteen. Never a reply. That means Matt (if that's his real name) (a) chatted with several girls, and I got lost in the mix; (b) simply forgot to reply; or (c) had a girlfriend and looked for easy, breezy girls. Either way, sometimes chatting annoyed me to no end.

I hate modern dating, with trends appearing out of nowhere. We've all heard of ghosting, breadcrumbing, haunting, whelming, benching, stashing, phubbing, and submarining. Submarining is similar to ghosting, only then, like, two weeks later, the guy appears as if nothing's happened, floating on the surface like a submarine: "Hey, what's up?"

I feel sorrow for the future of dating. In texting lingo, the gloom you experience could be expressed like a sad-looking face made out of a colon and a slash:

:/

I wasn't giving up, though, even if I felt absolutely discouraged. The current math was as follows: two out of three guys would post blurry pictures of themselves (sketchy) or would have that look of being a mommy's boy (no, thanks). Since I had no mom, my date didn't deserve a mom either—despite how selfish that sounds.

Overweight guys seemed eager and sweet; underweight guys were overly privileged; and buff, muscular guys were straight-up douchey.

I only wonder what men discuss behind our backs! Insert an angry emoji here made out of mathematical signs.

>_<

Six

Four weeks had magically flown by, bringing a surprisingly hot and humid end of May. Tulips seemed to enjoy the weather, and people had planted them in their little gardens if such were available. Trees and shrubs flourished, hiding houses in their viridity.

I love new beginnings, but especially the beginning of summer. After Memorial Day, something magical happens in the air. You'll be swept away by romance, or a new opportunity will come along. After a long winter and an even longer spring, you want to strip off the extra layers and go tanning at the beach—to show off that body you worked so hard for.

On Monday, June first, I woke up with back pain as usual. I'd been using an inflatable mattress, graciously provided by the furniture store of Lisa and Lise. The mattress often deflated, and the lack of sleep took its toll on my back and mental health.

I was cranky.

While working as a nanny on the Upper East Side, I got used to sitting and sleeping on plush, expensive, comfortable furniture. Now my back was killing me.

I refused to purchase an entire bed to save money. After all, my fund was being drained in the expected ways, starting with rent for May and June. Then I paid utilities and bought some clothes, groceries, coffee, cocktails, and green juices sold for ten bucks a pop downstairs. I now had $23,000, which meant I'd spent two grand in one month. When it came to the air mattress, I'd wake up feeling fantastic some days, thinking the mattress was tolerable, and other days, every bone hurt.

That day, my crinkly bones proved I needed to allow myself to splurge on a bed. I found Lisa in the living room, working by the window at her desk. On autopilot, I made a cup of matcha tea and plopped on the couch.

"Do you know where I can buy a cheap bed?" I asked Lisa, who was typing something really fast on her laptop.

"Look up this store on Steinway and Thirty-Sixth Avenue called Lyon's. Lise and I purchased our beds there."

"Great, thank you," I said and unlocked my phone.

"Do you wanna go out with Lise and me for a glass of wine in the evening?" she asked, eyes fixed on the screen, fingers typing. I wondered if Lisa had previously been a stenographer.

"I have a date in the evening, or otherwise I would."

"Look at you, lucky. Date after date."

"After the misogynist and the kleptomaniac, I'm dreading meeting anyone else. James is a runner. I'm, like, praying he's different."

"Can I see his picture?"

"Sure. The pictures are a little blurry, though," I said and stood up, showing her James's profile.

"Cute," she said, flipping through his photos. "How long have you been talking?"

"Like, two weeks."

"Good luck. I've also talked to him."

"You *did*?"

"But it didn't go anywhere. I believe he wasn't interested in me. Hopefully, you'll have more luck."

"Lisa, are you sure? I don't have to go out with him if that'll make you uncomfortable."

"Oh, it's totally fine. I didn't take his rejection personally. *The Four Agreements*," she said, referring to the self-help book that promoted not taking things personally. "Have you finished it, by the way?"

"Oh yes, long ago. Sorry, I meant to return it to you."

"It's OK. We need to discuss it. The author is going to be on Oprah's *SuperSoul Sunday*. We should all watch it."

"For sure," I said.

Our conversation dwindled to household talk, and then Lisa received a phone call, and I went for a jog.

Before going to the furniture store, I put in ten miles until my hamstrings were on fire, stretched in my bedroom with the air conditioner blasting, and showered.

I stopped at the café downstairs for an iced latte. While waiting in line to pay, I realized I'd been feeling so happy and absentminded since my run, a fa-la-dee-la-la kind of mood. My energy was through the roof, and my back stopped hurting. But I was still adamant about buying a spring mattress. Just because it no longer hurt, it didn't mean the pain wouldn't return.

I checked myself out in the mirror behind me. A baseball cap, glasses, booty shorts, flip-flops. A cropped tee that exposed my stomach and belly piercing. I loved the "I woke up like this" effect. Cute and casual. I paid for my latte and noticed how a guy in line checked me out while I checked myself out. I smiled from the absurdity of my vanity, and he smiled. I quickly remembered I'd seen him before at the gym and had nicknamed him Bun for his man-bun. He had scruff, which I love on a guy, and while he wasn't muscular per se, his mauve tank top revealed biggish arms with tattoos, which I also love. He was sweaty, probably after a workout. I gave him a look like I'd see him again.

The store Lisa suggested was located in an industrial part of Astoria, where auto shops and construction businesses had taken over, residential walk-ups lurking behind. Across Steinway Street, I saw an empty parking lot with a movie theater on one side and P.C. Richard on the other.

When I walked into Lyon's that day, something unexpected and magical happened. A girlfriend of mine once said that when she saw her future husband for the first time, she knew he was the one right away. (Yes, Chyna is annoying, but that's not the point.) That afternoon, I found the one. Only the one that I found was not a man. It was a job.

That afternoon was the beginning of how I would forever perceive happiness. And my life changed drastically.

Part Two

Cinnamon

You either walk inside your story and own it, or you stand outside your story and hustle for your worthiness.

—BRENÉ BROWN

Seven

Lyon's was a narrow, four-story structure at the end of Thirty-Sixth Avenue, nondescript and hard to find unless you were looking for it the way I did. Next to Lyon's, there were several auto shops, a tile store, and an accounting firm. A Mexican restaurant stood across the street. Northern Boulevard culminated Astoria, and on the opposite side of the street was Sunnyside, car dealerships and storage facilities running alongside.

I love jogging because it helps me explore. I recalled running near Lyon's, and this whole area gave me the creeps. Smashed cabs with open hoods were all over the place, some with windows cracked, some with doors missing. Mechanics in baggy, greasy pants roamed around. Ahead, a bridge connected Astoria to Sunnyside, a row of train tracks running underneath. This transitional area between the two communities was mostly desolate of people and probably dangerous at night. Manhattan skyscrapers were visible in the distance, a view that would soon be covered by the high-rises of the gentrifying neighborhood, Long Island City.

The door to Lyon's was propped open by a brick, so I walked in. Since the building stood in an unfortunate spot, covered by taller buildings from every direction, natural sunlight was hard to come by. Artificial lighting fixed the problem, but the light fell down in bizarre spots, without much thought.

The walls of the showroom were exposed brick, a décor not abundantly found in stores around the area. If done correctly, including better lighting, exposed brick showrooms are perfect spots for art exhibitions or fancy ateliers, with pop music playing on the radio and hip, young people roaming throughout.

Instead, the Lyon's showroom was a dumping ground of furniture. No structure whatsoever. Couches, armchairs, and coffee tables nestled close together, inseparable as if a waddle of penguins on an icy island, faux leather in black and brown.

I checked out the price tag on one of the couches. Two thousand dollars. *Jesus,* I thought. *Why did Lisa send me here?* Wooden coffee tables in lacquered black reflected artificial light from above. I saw my reflection in the glossy sheen.

According to an oversize sign, mattresses were located on the second floor, accessible via a staircase ahead. A girl with red hair was hustling with a box at the end of the showroom. Next to her stood a desk with a computer.

Two middle-aged men in tracksuits with thick, Eastern European faces were lounging on a couch, one of them talking on the phone in a language I couldn't place while the other one checked me out, his eyes following me uncomfortably like a hawk seeking prey. I remembered seeing an expensive car parked out front, which probably belonged to them. These were the type of men who frequented Cookie's strip club, wearing tracksuits, flashing pricey jewelry, and riding in expensive cars. Most of them European. That's why I was jealous of Europeans sometimes—because they take dating seriously, unlike American men, who find dating distracting.

As my browsing route came near the girl with red hair, I gave her a smile. We remained about ten feet away from each other, and my jaw dropped. I halted, stupefied for a moment, unable to believe who stood in front of me. A hallucination caused by a chronic lack of sleep?

I couldn't believe the girl was her, mainly because Cinnamon had moved away to Florida, deleted her social media, and vanished without a trace. Nobody knew where she was. She was the last person I expected to find at Lyon's.

But she was definitely Cinnamon.

Once you meet someone like her, you can't unmeet her. That's Cinnamon: she's dashing, with a chin dimple; large, gorgeous blue eyes; freckles just barely visible around the nose; fake lashes; microbladed eyebrows; and breasts she paid money for. Not once had I seen Cinnamon without French tips, and today was no exception, her nails glistening.

Cinnamon wore a cropped blue blouse and white linen pants. Even if her feet remained out of sight, I assumed she wore high heels. An assumption. As far as I knew, the soles of her feet had never touched the ground.

My legs carried me in her direction, for I was a gale, unaware of my surroundings, moved by purely animal instincts. I felt pain in my shin and noticed, belatedly, I'd hit a brown leather ottoman, spilling coffee on it.

When Cinnamon noticed me, she made a face, and we screamed in disbelief. After years of not seeing or talking to each other, the encounter seemed highly unlikely. She reached for a hug, and we finally grasped each other tightly, like a lid over Tupperware. I tasted her cologne on my tongue, subtle and woodsy. Cinnamon must have recently dyed her roots, burning auburn red, and the hair gleamed just like her nails, the smell of peroxide vague but discernible.

"Cinnamon, is that really you?" I squeaked, squeezing her as tightly as I could.

"Chardonnay!" she said in a low, smoker's voice, looking me up and down. "I can't believe it's you."

"What are you doing in Astoria? I tried finding you on social media, but you vanished from the face of the earth."

"I have new social media now. I needed distance from some toxic friendships, if you know what I mean."

"Yeah, totally." By toxic friendships, I assumed she meant crackhead girls from Cookie's strip club.

The baby fat had dissipated from her cheeks, and she was wearing smoky eye shadow, which she'd taught me how to apply. Her face glowed and was tight, full of Botox and fillers. Although Cinnamon was four years older, her forehead was smoother than a baby's butt. Mine, on the other hand, had started to get faint lines. I checked out her feet. Like I initially thought, she wore five-inch heels. She told me once, "If your feet don't hurt, don't even bother."

"What are you doing in Astoria?" I asked again.

"I worked at Cookie's for a bit when I returned from Florida."

"Oh right—I forgot you were from Florida too."

"How could you forget, Chardonnay? We bonded because we both grew up in Miami."

"I'm from Orlando."

"Oh right."

"So you're back for good?"

"Ew, not at all. New York is for losers. I'm just building a nest before I migrate to Key West with the birds. You know what I'm saying?"

"Totally," I said. "So you work here?"

"Yes, can you believe it? Aspen works here, too, actually."

"Aspen? I thought she also moved away."

"Girl, I helped Aspen return from Seattle."

"Why?"

"She lived there with some abusive asshole, so I pulled her out. She doesn't have any relatives otherwise. I was her only hope."

"Now I remember—she's a single child," I said. "Because I am too. I remember she traveled for a while."

"She actually lived with me in Miami, then disappeared in Nowhere, California, which is how the ding-dong ended up in Seattle. *Now* she's put for good. That is, until we move back to Florida in a few years. Key West."

"Why Key West?" I asked.

"Why not?"

"I mean, what's in Key West?"

"The sun, drinks … life? New York is for educated, overprivileged assholes. I'm here to save up, and then I'm out of here."

"How long have you worked at Lyon's?"

"A year now."

"I moved to Astoria at the beginning of May. I'd been working as a live-in nanny on the Upper East Side but quit. I'm trying to find something local."

"Why'd you quit?"

Somehow, I was ashamed to admit that I was looking for happiness. Cinnamon hated wishy-washy sentiments, and I imagined her saying, "You're looking for happiness? Get real, girl. Happiness is for assholes."

So I lied, "The dad couldn't keep his hands off me."

"I wouldn't keep my hands off you either," Cinnamon said. "Look at your gorgeous body. You're so skinny, bitch. Do you even eat?"

"I'm a runner now."

"Oh, fuck you. You're so young, a slice of pizza melts on your tongue with your stupid metabolism. I'm so jealous."

We started laughing then, and an older lady with a scarf wrapped around her head approached us.

"Excuse me, do you work here?" she asked me.

"No, I don't," I said.

"How much is that couch in black?" she asked me, pointing.

"Ma'am, there's a price tag on the arm," Cinnamon told her.

"I can't see the tag," the woman said.

"It's probably out of your price range anyway," Cinnamon said. "Our couches are, like, five thousand dollars and up."

"What's that?" the woman said. "I can't hear very well."

Cinnamon whispered to me, "Oh my God. Old crones like her come in every day with a budget of three dollars. Just a waste of my time."

"It's ten thousand dollars," Cinnamon said loudly.

"Ten thousand dollars?" the woman asked, incredulous.

"Perhaps you're better off somewhere else."

The woman crisscrossed her chest and moved along.

Cinnamon turned back to me. "Anyway. How you been, girl? I missed you."

I wasn't sure how sincere she was, but only one reply was appropriate—because I knew it was true: "I missed you, too, Cinnamon."

"We need to catch up, like, yesterday. What are you doing right now for work?"

"I'm looking for a job, actually."

"Where?"

I decided not to bore her with my cornerstones of happiness, how I was searching for an important vocation. Instead, I said, "Any job that doesn't involve children."

Cinnamon jumped, which scared me, so I jumped too.

"What the hell?" I asked.

She was laughing. "I didn't mean to scare you. I just realized that you should work here with Aspen and me."

I paused, and a chuckle escaped my mouth. How funny. Then I realized Cinnamon was serious.

"Wait, you for real?"

"Totally, girl."

"Doing what?"

"Selling furniture. What else? You're paid cash, so you don't pay taxes. It's a win-win situation. Plus, a commission from every sale."

I laughed, thinking that Cinnamon and cash had never separated, an eternal union. It was a strip club all over again.

"Why no taxes?" I asked. "Is the job illegal or something?"

"Taxes are so high in New York, and the owner, Lyon, wants to make sure we're getting a fair share. Fuck taxes. If I paid them, they would be thirty-three percent. Who can live on that shit? Unless, Chardonnay, you work for the damn IRS. In which case, I'll bury you in my basement."

"No, I love it," I said. "I didn't realize you could find a cash-paying job anymore, except at a strip club."

Cinnamon leaned closer and whispered, "The owner is obsessed with pretty girls. Obviously, I mean, that's why *I'm* here. When I pulled Aspen from Seattle, I brought her here."

"Who's the owner?"

"His name is Lyon."

"That's quite a name."

"Right? His family is originally Japanese, but he was born here. His real Japanese name is hard to pronounce, so he calls himself Lyon. But he doesn't look like a lion, girl. He looks like a goose."

"Is he ugly?"

"Yeah, a fat shmuck. He's not that bad-looking, but his jokes and personality make him worse. Thank God he's never here, or I'd murder him."

"How old is he?"

"I don't know. Like, fifty, maybe."

"So where is he if he's not at the store?"

"Usually travels a lot to Atlantic City. Gambling."

"Is he married?"

"Yes, but I've never seen the old hag. Anyway, he's here today, so let's get you hired, girl."

"Wait, right now?"

"He's never here. Might as well do it now."

"That's unexpected," I said. "How much does it even pay?"

"Smile, bitch, and take that damn hat off. I told you the pay is good."

Eight

While Cinnamon was fetching Lyon from upstairs, I browsed around the first floor, getting the feel of the place. If the bedroom stuff was located on the second floor, I wondered what was on the third and fourth floors. The men in tracksuits stood up and left, leaving me alone with the old lady in a headscarf. She was unable to see well, leaning toward each price tag.

My mind wandered to Cinnamon. After many years apart from a person, the brain erases any negative memories, the hard drive reformatted and ready for fresh files. Humans are quick to forget what hurt them in the past, which is good, I suppose—unless you get hurt again, in which case: shame on us.

But when it comes to happy memories, the brain keeps those memories intact. The two of us had fought a million times, but that day at Lyon's, I was left with a warm feeling inside, unable to remember a single argument. We'd once been close, Cinnamon and Chardonnay, and it'd hurt me when drugs escorted her in one direction while fate ushered me in another. She'd changed her number and blocked everyone from social media on a whim, an egoistic move on her part, careless and narcissistic, a thing a friend wouldn't do. She abandoned me, akin to my mom. She hadn't said goodbye—that's all the brain wants, a closure. I took it personally, and for years, I'd wanted to know what happened to her. At the time, she'd been going through a quarter-life crisis, always mad, moody, and mentally unstable. Frankly, I thought drugs had invited her to the other side years ago, which is why I couldn't believe she was back from the dead.

But none of that mattered anymore.

I also realized I'd never known her real name. Cookie, the house mom at the club, never allowed us to share our given names, whether with customers or with one another. Privacy aside, pseudonyms inspire mystery. I remember trying dozens of names for myself. First, they were precious stones: Ruby, Emerald, and Diamond. Then locations followed: Austin, Brooklyn, and Tennessee. I even tried colors, such as Jade, Teal, and Clementine—but nothing fit my personality. Cinnamon had suggested the name Chardonnay, and it instantly worked. (Last year, thanks to self-help books, I realized why I'd gone through thousands of names. I'd simply longed to find the name of my mother in the mix. That's, evidently, how our subconscious works.)

Cinnamon appeared on the staircase, holding the balustrade, her heels clicking.

"Lyon's taking the elevator, that fat slob," she told me.

"There's an elevator?" I asked. "Where?"

"Through that curtain."

Cinnamon pointed to a burlap curtain, which I'd noticed but didn't realize what it was for.

"There's a bathroom there as well," she said, "and an industrial-size elevator."

"How's there room for an elevator?"

"Listen, how are we going to move furniture up and down among the four floors?"

"I guess you're right."

"There's your new boss," Cinnamon sang in a higher tone.

A short, balding man appeared. He wore a white shirt, a red tie, and gray dress pants, no jacket. He resembled a businessman. His leather belt matched his leather shoes, black and lacquered, a watch and a gold chain. Some extra skin on his neck plopped out from the collar and hung loose as if he were a shar-pei. Lyon smiled when he noticed me and then waved. I'm not a waver, but I waved anyway. Wavers are the worst. I've never understood why I have such strong feelings against wavers, but when an old man waves like a little boy, it looks dumb.

He approached me, his eyes, black and without eyebrows, barely parallel to my shoulders. He looked up and said, "Hi, I'm Lyon," extending his hand for a handshake. His voice was higher than one would expect for a man his size, not quite helium-voice high, but close. I noticed a wedding band on his finger and two gold rings on the other hand, with diamonds all around them.

Swiftly, I moved my iced coffee from my right hand, wiped my palm against the back of my tee, and shook his hand.

"I'm Lindsay. Nice to meet you."

"My, my. Look what the cat dragged in. Cinnamon, you didn't tell me Lindsay was a model and blonde too. Quick, how much is three plus two? I'm joking. I actually don't think models are stupid. Besides, why do they need to know three plus two? Is that how many fingers are required to barf? What do you think?"

Cinnamon, behind him, rolled her eyes while looking at me and shook her head.

"I'm not sure," I said.

"That was a trick question, Lindsay, and you passed. You're looking for a job? You're hired. Cinnamon will explain everything else you need to know. She's my HR person and business manager. She hires and fires everyone."

"I *wish* I could hire and fire everyone," Cinnamon said. "Then I would fire Ichika."

"Cinnamon doesn't like my wife's sister working here," Lyon told me.

"It's not that I dislike like her per se, Lyon. She's sixty. It's time to retire. Am I right, or am I right?"

Lyon said, "Ichika's got cancer, and she wants to work before she dies. What am I supposed to do?"

"Let her . . . die?" Cinnamon said.

"Exactly. So Ichika forgets a couple of things, but who cares? Makes my wife happy."

Yikes, I thought to myself. Who was this Ichika, and why hadn't Cinnamon mentioned her before?

"Can you start tomorrow?" he asked.

"Yes, sir," I said.

"Great. I'll be out of town for a few days, but when I'm back, I'd like to get to know you better," he said, winked, and turned to Cinnamon. "Cinnamon, where's my fucking pizza?"

"I've ordered it, Lyon. It should arrive in, like, ten minutes."

"I'm starved. Bring it up as soon as it gets here."

His phone rang, which he was holding in his left hand, and when he picked up, he answered in Japanese. He waved as he moved toward the elevator while I continued looking at Cinnamon.

"What the hell was that?" I asked.

"He's a little unhinged," she said. "Thankfully, he's never here, so you won't have to deal with him."

"I guess."

"Welcome to the team, Chardonnay!" she said in a sweet voice and reached for a hug. "I already texted Aspen, but the ding-dong is still asleep."

"He calls you by your nickname?"

"Cinnamon?" she asked.

"Yeah."

"That's my real name, girl."

"For real?"

"Well, for real as in *what*? I legally changed it years ago."

"From what?"

"From something I clearly don't wanna discuss, or otherwise, I wouldn't have changed it, Chardonnay."

"Got it," I said. "Who is Ichika?"

"She's his wife's sister, and she's also from Japan. I can barely understand when she speaks, like a Japanese radio station with her gibberish shit."

"Where is Ichika today?"

"It's her day off. She always takes Mondays off after busy weekends. The good news is, Aspen and I get most weekends off."

"So she's here by herself?"

"Sometimes. Other times, Aspen or I will be here with her. I mean, we get our flat rate of three hundred bucks per day. It doesn't matter if we're here all day or not. Only if we sell something—then we get a commission. But even without it, girl, the pay is good."

"Sounds a little sketchy, to be honest. I know what it takes to work for cash. Something else must be involved." *Like drugs,* I implied but avoided saying.

"Relax, Chardonnay. I'd never put you in a position that could jeopardize you in any way. Lyon overprices the furniture now and then, and Ichika is the only person on the payroll, so it looks good for the books. But we don't pay taxes, and that money goes straight into our pockets, which is the best deal for us. Don't worry, Miss IRS. We don't do anything illegal here if that's what you mean."

I chuckled, thinking the three of us would be working together again—Aspen, Cinnamon, and Chardonnay—on stage, a.k.a., the showroom. Three hundred dollars a day added up to $6,000 per month. Cash. I still didn't understand who would pay for ugly faux-leather furniture, but heck, it was on them if people paid.

"Chardonnay," she said, "let's celebrate tonight."

"I wish I could, but I have a date in the evening."

"Cancel."

"I can't. I was really looking forward to meeting him. Plus, I've already canceled twice."

"All right."

"How about tomorrow evening after work?"

"Tomorrow evening sounds good. I'm so excited," she said. "But come here at nine in the morning. It'll just be you and me. And then we'll celebrate after work."

"OK."

We hugged and exchanged phone numbers, and off I went. On my way home, she texted me a picture of a cinnamon stick with, *"Hi, this is me."*

I sent her a bottle of chardonnay. *"And this is me."*

Nine

On the way home, I couldn't stop smiling from happiness. Had I really just found a job within walking distance where I'd work with friends? No taxes meant saving even more money.

Deep inside, I knew the job was not a "meaningful vocation," but somehow, it no longer mattered. I felt incredible happiness, and that's what mattered. Working together in the past had connected us, magnet Cinnamon and steel Chardonnay. I felt that butterfly feeling people experience when they fall in love. Goosebumps, weak knees. Isn't this special feeling that makes you elated the exact definition of happiness? Maybe the third cornerstone lay not in the significance of work per se, but in the butterflies?

I showered, got ready for my date, and to help with courage, poured a glass of cold white wine before venturing out for the evening.

Cinnamon was going down memory lane and kept texting me photos from our club days with comments. "*God, what are you wearing here?*" Or "*I remember this Halloween like yesterday. God, was I drunk.*"

I had no idea somebody cared enough to save them, and I smiled. In my quarter-life-crisis rage, I'd erased that part of my past, along with all its memorabilia—for good.

Thankfully, Cinnamon was not as impulsive during hers, preserving not only her memories but mine as well.

In one picture, I was still Jade, with a short black wig and bangs, clutching a pole in undergarments. I looked hideous, I thought. In another picture, I was Austin, with a shoulder-length razor cut, dirty blonde. Cinnamon had never changed her auburn hair, but she looked different in the photos, pre-fillers and young. She kept changing her wardrobe throughout the years, trying to find her style, but never missed a pair of heels. Blue eyes, a chin dimple—Cinnamon was always a knockout, Cookie's favorite girl. But today, she looked different, a classier Cinnamon 2.0—poised, confident. An adult. I wished to become that one day, sure of myself, calm, truly happy.

Lisa was watching TV in the living room by herself. The air conditioner was blasting on full while she stretched under a blanket on her (right) side of the couch. I've always found it strange when people do that—sit in a cold room covered up. Isn't that a plus and a minus, the air conditioner and the blanket? Lisa was such a Scorpio. In the desert, scorpions crawl out at night while the rest of the world is asleep, enjoying the freezing night air.

"I thought you and Lise were going out," I said and sat down on the other side of the couch.

She looked up. "Lise is running late. She had a showing at five, but the client mixed up the time. Did you buy a bed?"

"No, I didn't buy anything, but something much better happened. I walk into the furniture store, and there's this girl, the saleswoman, who looks so familiar. Turns out, I know her. Her name is Cinnamon. We used to work together at a—"

"Strip club?"

"Yes, but how did you know?"

"With a name like Cinnamon, I just assumed."

"Yeah," I said, taking in my sudden embarrassment. Somehow, even mentioning a strip club sounded dirty coming out of Lisa's mouth, a tad judgmental or something. "Can we refer to it as a club? *Strip club* has a weird connotation all of a sudden."

"I understand. I'll call it whatever you want me to call it, roomie," she said and smiled.

"OK. Anyway, so Cinnamon works there as a salesperson with Aspen, who's also from—"

"The strip club? Sorry. Name Aspen. I just assumed again. The club."

"Anyway," I said. "When I tell Cinnamon I'm looking for jobs, she's like, 'Well, look no more. We're hiring. Let me introduce you to Lyon, the owner.' So Lyon comes downstairs and tells me I resemble a model. What?" I asked Lisa, who was laughing.

"When you're excited, you babble like a little girl."

"I do? I didn't realize it. Sorry."

"No, it's funny."

"Lyon said I could start tomorrow. And Cinnamon said we're not supervised, most weekends are off, great pay, and even a commission. I've found a job that could become my cornerstone of happiness. Mission three accomplished."

I raised my wine glass to cheer symbolically and took a sip.

"Congratulations, roomie, but I believe you should consider other options."

"What options?"

"Do you sincerely wanna carry that baggage from the past and work with girls from a strip club? You can't even say 'strip club.'"

There she goes again, I thought. A freaking Scorpio who tells you how it is, whether you like it or not.

"It's not baggage, Lisa. We were friends back then, not the best friends, but we had a great time together."

"When was the last time you and Cinnamon talked?"

"Not sure, maybe five years ago."

"People change really fast. You don't know anything about anyone after . . . six months."

"I don't think that's true. Cinnamon is literally the same person she was before. Like a time capsule."

"I doubt working at Lyon's is a good idea, Lindsay. I think I know exactly who you're talking about. The girl with red hair?"

"Yes, that's Cinnamon."

"I'm not crazy about her. I went there two weeks ago, hopped in after the movie with Lise to look at some desks. That Cinnamon girl acted like I couldn't afford anything. So judgmental, that one."

"She wasn't judging. She told me many customers who come in can't afford the furniture. Today there was this lady who couldn't afford a couch, and Cinnamon knew it. Why waste our time?"

"That's like a scene from *Pretty Woman*. Big mistake on her part."

"I've never seen that movie," I said.

"Just think about it before you jump in."

"I mean, I can always quit. I'm not on the books or anything. They pay cash."

"Cash?" Lisa barked. "You're not even on the payroll?"

"No. Cinnamon said Lyon pays us cash to help us avoid paying thirty-something percent on taxes."

"That doesn't sound like a true intention. After the twenty-oh-eight financial crisis, I learned one lesson: if your boss pays you cash, that's sketchy."

"Why is it sketchy?"

"Because if you get injured at work and spend the rest of your life in a wheelchair, you won't receive any justice by suing anyone. You're nonexistent, like a ghost, and replaceable, like a rubber glove."

"It's a small operation, Lisa, and they don't need an accountant. Cinnamon is the HR, Lyon said. It's like working with family and friends. You don't need to sue one another."

"I love you, which is why I'm not crazy about you working there."

Lisa sounded so condemnatory, as usual, and I could no longer take it. I learned from self-help books the difference between a jerk and a friend who gives advice: advice is solicited. It seemed unbelievable that Lisa was already shitting on a job I hadn't even started.

"I have to continue getting ready for my date," I lied and went to my room. I wondered why Lisa was being unsupportive. Was she mad at me for going on a date with James? Being an accountant wasn't an excuse to act like a "see you next Tuesday."

I texted Lise and Liam about finding a job, both of whom failed to reply. Then I texted Nikita, knowing she'd be happy for me for sure.

Nikita texted back: "*Congrats!*" Which was followed by a GIF of Patrick Star from *SpongeBob SquarePants* clapping and saying, "Congratulations."

All I got was Patrick Star, after struggling to find a job for a month? A "congrats"? I knew her café, the nurse job, and Joaquin kept her on her toes, but I deserved more than a "congrats" and a GIF.

Chloe, an evil Aquarius, held a grudge about the nanny job. She'd never forgive me and would be unhappy to hear my good news. And Candace would turn the tables and start discussing vaginas. Instead of contacting them, I poured more wine and resumed reading a self-help book by Tosha Silver called *Outrageous Openness.* The author suggests this incredible idea: if we're completely, utterly open to whatever life may bring, it will happen; we just have to be open to it. In a sense, the book may be an extension to *The Secret*, which deals with the law of attraction. We're told over and over again that we get what we wish for. Was I subconsciously attracting people like Lisa, Chloe, and Candace into my life? Because if that was true, I subconsciously evoked punishment to myself. Lisa clearly cared little for my feelings, Chloe only cared about her mental health, and Candace annoyed me with her transgender stuff. I was a magnet for people who wanted to belittle me somehow, a dumping ground for others' hatred.

I decided to stop being a pushover—starting that evening. *Nobody,* I promised myself, *will take advantage of me.* I'd been pleasing everyone at my own expense, but what happened in the end? In the end, I had no friends left who genuinely seemed happy for me. Mine only cared about their own selfish agendas.

I could guarantee everybody respected Cinnamon because she spoke her mind. And while typically I avoided confrontation, that day, I provoked my friends. I had to receive the respect I deserved. Anger triggers anger, and if I hadn't had a fight with Lisa, I would never have rubbed my job in Chloe's face.

I texted Chloe and Candace, channeling Cinnamon: *"Yo, bitches. I finally found a job after a whole month!"*

Candace replied: *"Nice. I still need help finding a surgeon. I'm sure Dr. Stern will sign my papers soon. You've been so neglectful of me. I'll never be happy until I'm a woman with a vagina!"*

What kind of response was *that*? Candace's happiness always seemed conditional. With her, it was always, "I won't be happy until this or that." We met at a house party years ago for a former girlfriend of mine (from Cookie's strip club), and Candace was in law school. She's ten years older, and at the time, she was in her early thirties and struggling in school. Then it was, "I'll never be happy until I finish this dumb school." A year later, it was, "I won't be happy until I find a job." Now, "I won't be happy until I have a vagina." Maybe it was time to cut her off for good.

Chloe called, and I picked up, anger brewing inside me, black and strong like coffee.

"Hey," she said, "I'm so happy for you. One question: Do you plan to take every job in the city?"

"Chloe, don't be mad."

"Oh, how convenient. When Lindsay tells me not to be mad, I magically won't be."

"No sarcasm necessary."

"In my circle of friends, I'm the only one without a job."

"First of all, you don't have a circle of friends. It's just you because you can't stop complaining."

"What are you gabbing about? I have other friends, you know."

"Who? Candace? Candace who can't stop talking about her vagina? Or your other friend, weed?"

"What is your problem, Lindsay?"

"You blame me for everything."

"Don't you turn it around on me, missy. After I threw up at that house party six months ago, everyone started treating me differently."

"How do I treat you differently, Chloe?"

"You avoid me."

"It has nothing to do with you throwing up."

"Then what *is* it about?"

"I'm looking for happiness, Chloe, and as soon as I start putting another cornerstone in the ground, you arrive on a bulldozer, ready to destroy everything."

"How do I destroy your happiness?"

"For one, you blamed me for not offering you the nanny job, which I had no control over. And now you're unhappy that I've found a job. What do you want, Chloe? For the whole world to be miserable just to make you feel better?"

"You're lying to me. You're embarrassed by me. If I hadn't thrown up, you would have offered the nanny job to me."

"You know why I didn't offer you that stupid job? Because you're so freaking privileged."

"What the hell are you talking about?"

"Unlike many of us, you live with your mother in a home where you're welcome, and there's a huge inheritance from Daddy. You don't have to lift your pale white finger, but black people like Kitty must hustle just to put some food on the table. Just because you're bored out of your stupid mind—creating lies and stories in your head that everyone hates you—it doesn't mean they're true. You got that, privileged girl?"

Chloe was sobbing. "I hope you throw up at a party or get fat or something, and we'll see who's privileged then. You only see what you wanna see, a privileged white girl. Well, you're white too. Don't make it a racial issue."

"I offered that job to Kitty because she has two mouths to feed. If you put your word out there, people will give you whatever you want, Chloe."

"I have been putting the word out there!"

"Where? When complaining to me on the phone?"

"So what are you saying?"

"That you're either lazy or you simply don't wanna work."

Silence. I looked at the phone, but she'd hung up. I was livid and yet felt bad for calling her lazy. Perhaps it was time to cut her off for good, just like Candice. I'd gained two friends from the past, Aspen and Cinnamon, so losing two, Chloe and Candace, was (at least) mathematically correct. I wished I hadn't become this annoyed and agitated before my date. Everyone blamed me for something. They were jealous, I concluded—simple as that.

I ran to the kitchen, poured myself another glass of wine, and realized I'd finished the bottle—by myself in one evening. Using a funnel, I poured the last glass back into the bottle and set it in the fridge, thinking I'd had enough anyway. So strange that when you're mad, you want to get drunk.

Ten

I was already fashionably late for my date (which means ten minutes). We'd made plans to meet at 6:00 p.m. at a hip wine bar that served pretentiously small appetizers. It was on Thirty-Third Street, just two blocks down. Being late was inexcusable but also absolutely necessary. I may be a feminist, but I also play by the rules: men must be on time, and women should be late. To show we're not desperate. After polishing off three glasses of wine by myself, I realized, belatedly, I should have canceled. My flirty side had come out, which meant that if I drank any more, I'd be an easy target for James. I would not be myself. After all, my goal was to find a soulmate, but I was barely in a soulmate mood. Instead, I wanted to flirt and be told how tan, skinny, and beautiful I looked. I wanted to be kissed and caressed. One guy passing me on the street did a double take, approving my first-date "it's humid and the beginning of June," easy-breezy-CoverGirl outfit: a mauve midi wrap dress, black three-inch heels, and a clutch. My hair was down, no makeup, just some eyeliner and nude lip gloss.

James should say, "You look amazing in that outfit!"

And I should reply, "Oh, please, this old rag?"

While I showed some décolletage, but my cleavage was not on display. I wasn't Mona Lisa at the Louvre—if that's where the *Mona Lisa* is. I really don't know.

The sun was crawling toward the horizon, coloring Astoria ablaze with gorgeous orange hues. A day full of sunshine had left the sidewalk throbbing with intense heat, and I felt like I was inside a steam room. My armpits instantly dampened, and only an air conditioner could fix me. Thirtieth Avenue teemed with people, most of whom were returning from work in the city. Sidewalk cafés and restaurants hosted dinner crowds, a dozen bars on the way full of happy-hour girls. Happy hours in Astoria lasted from 5:00 p.m. until the last girl standing. They were laughing, and the music was playing. It always feels incredible to be a part of a big group—socialize, be flirted with, share ideas with other people. Maybe that's why Lisa was so bitter earlier, I thought, projecting her anger at me. She was home all alone, a grumpy old crone under a grandmother's blanket, while young girls were taking over the world.

Well, screw Lisa.

I stopped on the corner before the bar to freshen up my memory of what James looked like. In one of his pictures, he wore running gear, and in another, a New York City Marathon bib, looking handsome, which means the photo was blurry. Runners are typically good-looking and on the skinnier side. James was a biggish guy with thick calves and thick black hair.

Killer smile.

Five eleven.

Thirty-one.

I looked in the selfie camera to ensure nothing weird had gotten stuck in my hair, no seeds in my teeth. Great. I looked good and felt confident—time to get flirty.

Jazz music and the aroma of french fries welcomed me when I opened the door to the bar.

I noticed James right away, realizing the carpet didn't match the drapes. Which means his pictures didn't match reality. We, as humans, should know our best or at least kind of cute angles. James did not. I noticed him instantly, a single guy in a bar full of groups and couples. He slouched sideways in the middle of the bar, belly popping out through the buttons of his flannel shirt. Who wears flannel on a hot summer day and in the summer in general? With jeans! How, first of all, was he not hot? I walked two blocks and was sweating more than Kris Jenner before STD testing. And second of all, jeans are basic, and I expected a little more from him. Even the kleptomaniac and the misogynist had put more consideration into their outfits. Especially the misogynist, who was really handsome. I suddenly wished I was on a date with him instead. At least I'd had a handsome face to look at, even if his hands repeatedly slid toward my knee.

Boy, had James transformed from his runner days. I was maybe ten feet away from him, taking him in without getting seen, as James was gazing at his phone. He was balding, chubby, and sporting a goatee. If I could tolerate a trait, a goatee it wasn't. A goatee was a real deal-breaker. In general, a goatee looks too fake or too manicured or too something, and I adore guys who "just woke up like this"—who look dapper without seemingly trying. But dapper James wasn't. This is the box that James failed to check:

☐ No goatee.

Suddenly, a goatee wasn't the worst. Do I even dare to share? James was nervously tapping his foot against the stool, and I noticed he wore brown-strapped sandals, exposing his toes. You read that right: toes. Another failed box:

☐ No sandals. Toes closed at all times on a date.

Tomorrow, Cinnamon would say, "Nuh-uh! No way, girl. Who would do such a stupid thing?"

When you come to Uruguay, do what Uruguayans do, and when you go on a date, never, under any circumstances, wear sandals.

I turned around 180 degrees and reached for the door hidden behind a curtain to keep the cold air from escaping. This was when I heard James calling my name: "Lindsay?"

Nope, I thought to myself, finding this amusing. I wasn't Lindsay at the moment—I was Cinnamon. That's the effect she had on everybody. The minute you meet her, you're obsessed, and impersonation is the sincerest form of flattery.

The door in front of me flew open, with five young, tipsy guys trying to enter without letting me exit. They pushed me so far back, I realized fate had won, and I had to meet him. I stretched a smile, turned, and pretended to scan the bar as if searching for him. When I finally "found" James by fixing my eyes on him, I squinted as though trying to decide whether it was him. Feeling like a fool, I quickly waved, the way Lyon had that afternoon, and James waved back.

"Hi, are you James? I'm Lindsay."

What happened next was even more cringy and embarrassing than goatees and sandals.

"Hi, nice to meet you," James said, extending his hand.

His elbow accidentally met a beer bottle, and it fell, banging against the bar. Without missing a beat, James grabbed the neck of the bottle, which was full of foam, and tried to position it upright. Instead, the slippery bottle somersaulted in the opposite direction, with the neck of the bottle facing him. The beer jumped toward his jeans like kids to a trampoline.

Eleven

"At which point, this is a commotion, and people are staring," I told Lisa. "This bartender girl appeared with a towel and wiped the bar. James started blotting his crotch with napkins. *So* awkward. I'm standing nearby, a fool, feeling embarrassed for a guy who doesn't look like his pictures *at all.* James is conducting this apologetic chitchat, right? But I'm so humiliated, I'm not even listening to him. The bartender reassures him all is fine, and I pretend I'm on Neptune or some planet far away."

"And?" Lisa asked impatiently. "You ditched him?"

"Not ditched him, per se. I told him to close the tab and tip the bartender triple. 'I'll wait outside,' was all I said, then I left the bar, blocking his profile."

I was drinking the leftover wine, finishing the bottle, and Lisa opened a pinot noir for herself. While I was out for twenty minutes on my date, she'd prepared a cheese board with crackers and fig jam, and I made an hors d'oeuvre, mixing all three.

"I don't understand," Lisa said. "You freaked out because the guy wore sandals? What's wrong with sandals?"

"Everything is wrong with sandals."

"Like what?"

"I could see his toes."

"So what?"

"That's inappropriate."

"How is it inappropriate?"

"I don't know. It's just a dating rule."

"I've lived in New York my entire life, and I've never heard of that rule."

"Don't you think after all the time I'd spent getting ready, he could've at least put some socks on and regular shoes?"

"Nobody asked you to spend hours getting ready for a date. That was your choice. You wanted to show off."

"I wasn't showing off. What's wrong with looking good? Plus, I didn't want to waste an evening with a guy I was going to hate."

"You don't know that. Maybe he's great."

"If he's so great, then you go out with him."

"Well, that's the point, Lindsay. I've tried to go out with him, but he doesn't go for people like me."

"Is that what this is about?" I asked. "That he chose me over you? I asked you about it, and you gave me your permission."

"It's not about that. It's more about respect. Like what do you think he's thinking right now? Like he's a sloppy moron?"

"He was."

"I feel bad for him."

"You *should* feel bad for him. He puts out old pictures to get dates. That's so pathetic."

"So you're saying your pictures are accurate?"

Flabbergasted at the insult, I answered with a question, "Are you serious, Lisa?"

"Your photos are edited, every zit removed, and full of filters."

"But at least they're my pictures."

"Yes, they're your pictures, but all that editing makes you look better. That's the exact definition of lying."

"You should see your photos, Lisa," I fired back. "At least I know my angles."

"At least mine are real."

"Oh, you want to get real, Lisa? At least guys in sandals click 'yes' on me, and I put myself out there, seeing sandals and all. You literally just sit here all day and judge everyone for your loneliness. Don't be jealous."

She laughed creepily, from the top of her throat. "Please. Unlike you, I don't need a relationship to define me. I don't need cornerstones of happiness. The perfect partner for me, instead of completing or competing, will complement me."

"That's self-help-book bullshit. You should turn off Oprah and get real."

"Get real about what?"

"You're bitter because you're almost forty, but you still live with four roommates, and nobody wants you. Maybe you should go out once in a while."

"There you go, carrying around your privilege like a purse."

"I've never been privileged, Lisa. I worked hard for what I have. Unlike you, Lise, and Liam, I don't have family in Delaware and Connecticut and upstate New York. I worked hard for my room, my body, and my money without anyone backing me up. So don't preach to me about being fake. And speaking of fake, what about those trash bags you leave outside for our neighbors? They take it down for you, thinking the trash is theirs. You just sit here, do nothing, and have others do all the work."

"Are you out of your mind?" she said. "Not only did it never bother you before, but I do everything around here. Just after you left the apartment, who do you think washed the funnel and the wine glass in the sink?"

"Unlike you, Lisa, I have a life, and I would've washed the dishes when I got back."

"Bullshit. You've never cleaned a single dish. I end up washing everything for you."

"That's because you never let me clean them—you expect everything to happen on your time clock, like I'm supposed to wash everything the minute I touch it. I come back, and everything is washed and put away."

"It's because I don't want any cockroaches. You should clean your plates as soon as you use them. That's how simple it is. And maybe get your hair out of the sink in the bathroom once in a while. And don't leave your heels all over the place."

"So now it's about me being messy?" I asked.

"You don't respect anyone. You take forever in the shower. People need to use it, too, you know. That's what this is about. You just continue showing your personality, which is a spoiled and privileged brat."

My eyes fell out of my head. "I don't need this," I said and got off the couch, finishing my wine in one sip.

I continued, "You're insulting my pictures and my dating choices. Then you sit there like a big fat liar. So *I'm* disrespectful when *you're* the one telling me I look fake in my pictures and that I'm supposed to date a guy who wears sandals. I'd rather go out with the misogynist."

"That's who you deserve."

Twelve

The next morning, I woke up hungover and disoriented, sunlight seeping through the cracks in my curtains. Last night, murky and alcohol infused, was slowly returning in flashes, and my head was pounding. I shrieked when I realized a guy was sleeping next to me.

Flashbacks fired. Right, it was the misogynist. Shot after shot at the bar.

"I thought I'd never see you again," the misogynist said, his hand in my underwear.

"Me neither."

More shots followed; his mouth reached for my mouth, his tequila breath. I was tasting lime and salt, and when our lips unmet, something crunchy was left in my mouth. I spewed it out on my palm, where I saw a kernel of corn, orange in the darkness.

"I didn't even eat corn today," I said drunkenly, laughing.

"It must've been from my dinner," he said.

The misogynist had consumed enough truth serum to start narrating all the fetishes that turned him on. He wanted to tie me up and spank me while I lay in bed, begging for mercy. I'd also learned he was into punishing women the first night we met. He had talked about his ex the entire time, suggesting women had been created for his pleasure and amusement. I hate that alcohol erases memories.

This is what I've learned from self-help books: As children, we learn about the system of "crime and punishment," and if we behave naughtily, adults punish us. Such a system turns tables on us. As adults, after insulting someone emotionally, even if we feel bad about it at the end, there's nobody to punish us. We're like, "Whoa, whoa, whoa, slow down. You're telling me that I can verbally abuse anyone, without repercussion? Oh wow, that's dangerous."

We punish others for every little mistake, committing emotional crimes like the criminals we are. However, the system of "crime and punishment" is so deeply engraved in us that we eventually break down.

Once we admit we've committed a crime, then what?

So now we must *punish* ourselves by feeling guilt and sometimes agony. At least as adults, we get the choice of forgetting our problems by drinking them away. But in a corner of the mind, the subconscious part still keeps the guilt on the back burner, and eventually, it will seek punishment for every wrongdoing, even a minor one. That's why we need to talk about our feelings, apologize if needed, and move on with the following attitude: "I'll do better next time."

After talking to Lisa, I felt terrible for ditching James. I hated to admit she was right. The least I could do was give him a chance after making plans and talking and wasting all that time. But instead of feeling bad and apologizing, I had contacted the woman-hater.

Boy, did he want to do lots of nasty things. Meeting men with fetishes wasn't anything new for me, especially after working at a strip club, where men with money assume anything goes. For the most part, that's true. While I respect all fantasies without judgment, fetishes aren't something I enjoy for myself. As soon as men realize you can be a toy, you'll be treated like one. Nasty, merciless, and degrading. Of course, sex is a weapon, and it helped me survive when I worked at the strip club. Cookie hadn't run a prostitution ring, but for the right price, I had to comply with her policies. "Special clients receive special treatments," Cookie would say. A dozen times, such VIP sadists left me blindfolded, tied up, and helpless, all in the name of realizing their fantasies.

To balance the planet, other men craved punishment instead. Feisty Cookie, large and in charge, enjoyed whipping submissive men in her boudoir, cashing out $3,000 per session. The thing about fetishes is that you can never tell what a man wants just by looking at him. Quiet, innocent doormats can be freaks in bed, and roaring lions will end up the biggest pussies.

In a boyfriend, however, I sought vanilla—as dull and conventional as possible. In fact, I sometimes wondered whether I enjoyed sex with a man to begin with, for time and time again, men kept disappointing me. Metaphorically speaking, who finds pleasure in two licks of ice cream, grunts, and throws the ice cream out?

The evening with the misogynist was murky, and memories jumbled without particular chronological order. I remembered us wrestling. I tried to prevent him from overpowering me, yet he managed to climb up anyhow and restrained my arms. He believed we were role-playing a fetish of his, a consensual rape fantasy to which no woman would agree. He kept shushing me with a palm against my mouth while I tried fighting him off, which only further turned him on. His hands of steel were ungiving, restraining a drunk and vulnerable girl who'd brought this onto herself, unable to put up much of a fight. I fidgeted and moaned while trying to escape. The misogynist was rock hard when he approached me, but he wasn't wearing a condom, which frightened me to no end. I pretended I was suffocating, which prompted him to free my mouth. In a drunken twang, I told him no sex without a condom. He was angry, and the anger only ignited him further. He inserted one or two fingers inside me, and with the other hand, he worked on himself. Somehow, it became peaceful, and I zoned out. When I opened my eyes, he was wiping sticky goo from my breasts.

Thirteen

With him snoring next to me, I found my phone, uncharged and almost dying on my nightstand. Cinnamon had called three times in the past hour. I dialed her back.

"Bitch, where are you?" was her opening. "You were supposed to be here an hour ago."

"What time is it?"

"It's ten thirty."

"Oh shit."

"Is everything OK?"

"I'm fine. I overslept."

"Take your time. Lyon isn't here today. Just me."

After I hung up, the next fifteen minutes seemed like a sitcom being fast-forwarded. The misogynist woke up after I repeatedly jerked his shoulder. I felt disgusted by his behavior the night before and avoided eye contact. Unhurriedly, he propped up against the wall and groaned.

"You must leave," I said.

"Why?"

"I'm late for work."

"Let's do a quickie."

"I don't have time for a quickie."

"Why not?"

"I need to get ready for work."

"I can be quick."

"I need to shower."

"Let's shower together."

"I said no."

In quick, shuddering gestures, he hopped inside his white shorts, the color contrasting with his tan skin. My eyes kept getting accustomed to the darkness, and I watched as he put on boat shoes and buttoned his Armani shirt, which he'd mentioned numerous times the night before to remind me how rich and fashionable he was.

He said, "Like, I bought all our drinks. The least you can do is quickly put out. You don't even have to do anything. You don't even have to move."

I couldn't believe the words coming out of his mouth. I was in so much pain from the hangover that I almost gave in. Sometimes it's easier to give the man what he wants to be left alone. Cinnamon would slap him instead and throw him through the window.

"We'll have sex next time," I lied.

"Yeah, whatever," he said and left.

Lisa was working by the window when I snuck into the bathroom to shower. Earlier that morning, Lise had taken a train to Washington, DC, for a real estate convention, leaving two dogs under the same roof unattended.

I showered at a rocket speed, threw something on in haste, and was out the door by eleven, my head pounding. Eighty degrees outside promised a warm, sunny day. As I walked, my stomach twisted into a knot from hunger, reminding me I'd skipped breakfast. Thirst joined the party. I detoured for an iced coffee and a green smoothie. At eleven thirty, two and a half hours late, I made it for my first day.

Fourteen

When Cinnamon noticed me entering the store, she rose to her feet, a smile with bright-red lipstick stretching across her face. Red is such a Leo color. She wore her hair away from her face in a ponytail, which was why the red lipstick stood out. Heels, obviously, and a jade suit with a black blouse. Next to her, I probably resembled a little girl, with my unruly, frizzy hair and mismatched outfit of pink linen pants and a striped blouse.

I approached the desk at the end of the showroom and spoke first. "I'm sorry I'm late. I overslept."

"You have time for coffee, ho, and you're two hours late?"

"I'm sorry, Cinnamon."

"I'm just joking around, girl. It's totally fine. What the hell happened last night? Didn't you say you had a date?"

"Oh, Cinnamon, it's such a long and complicated story."

"We literally have all day with nothing to do. Tuesdays are the slowest here. Tell me everything."

"Let me finish my coffee first."

Cinnamon reached out and plucked the sunglasses off my face, making me squint from the artificial brightness.

"Oh, girl," she said. "You weren't fucking kidding. You need to invest in some eyedrops. I use them every morning."

She opened a desk drawer, where she found a bottle of eyedrops.

"Now, tell me everything," she said.

I poured the drops in, which stung, and said, while rubbing my eyes, "My date showed up in sandals, and he spilled beer on his crotch as soon as we met."

Cinnamon's face underwent a contortion, and her jaw dropped exaggeratedly.

"The motherfucker showered up in sandals and was sloppy? What a moron."

"That's what I told Lisa, my roommate. Then she yelled at me for ditching his ass and said my pictures were fake."

"What pictures?"

"From the dating apps."

"Can I see?"

I pulled out my phone and opened my dating profile.

Cinnamon flipped through my photos, saying, "You look smokin' hot, girl. What the hell is Lisa gabbing about? She called you fake?"

"Yes."

"She's jealous, is all. Your pictures look outstanding. Chardonnay, you know how to take a good photo, and you know your angles."

"Thank you. Apparently, my roommate had matched with the sloppy shmuck, but he stopped replying to her. Which is why she's angry."

"How old is Lisa?"

"Like, thirty-seven, I think."

"Oh, no wonder. Old people are exactly like that. Dried up and jealous. Wait until you meet the sixty-six-year-old Ichika."

"Who's Ichika?"

"The woman who works here."

"Oh right. The Japanese woman with cancer."

"Yes, Lyon's wife's sister."

"What about her?"

"She reminds me of your roommate. She lost her opportunities years ago, and now she's absolutely nuts."

"In what way?"

"She's just not … fully there, if you know what I mean."

"Like, mentally ill?"

"She's just weird. She gave up on herself years ago. She snacks on these disgusting sunflower seeds, and they get stuck all over her teeth. Then she goes and talks to customers. I just *can't* with her."

"I see."

"By the way, Aspen is off today, but I told her to meet us at Randy's after work. We're going to close early, at six. It's literally just you and me here today."

"What's Randy's?"

"Our watering hole on Forty-Fourth Street and Thirty-First Avenue."

"I don't think I can drink after last night."

"Oh, you will. I got you a job, and we need to celebrate."

Fifteen

Work, if you could call it that, comprised following Cinnamon around the store, getting "the feel of the place." There was nothing to feel, in my opinion. For the next hour, not one single person walked through the door, which allowed me to explore.

The second floor was similar to the first, in that beds and mattresses were crammed together, without order. From one point of view, I understood the logic behind it. Astoria provided limited space for a giant furniture store—we weren't at an IKEA. But if they removed just three beds and spaced out the rest of the furniture, it would make a world of difference. Signs welcomed guests to try the mattresses, and I lay on one, trying it out. After all, I still needed to purchase a bed. Soft, medium, or firm?

"What are you doing, girl?" Cinnamon asked.

I laughed because I didn't realize she'd followed me here. "I came in yesterday to buy a bed."

"Don't buy this overpriced piece of shit. Here—follow me."

Cinnamon offered her hand to help me get up and held my hand in hers the entire time, until we approached a different mattress.

"Try it," she said.

I plopped down, noticing the mattress failed to bounce and felt hard against my back.

"What do you think?" she asked.

"Hard."

"You need hard, Chardonnay. Soft mattresses damage the spine."

"Is that true?"

"Totally."

She lay down next to me and said, "It's yours for free."

"What? How come?"

"Merchandising. Lyon doesn't know that I overcharge certain customers sometimes, which ends up in a surplus."

"For real?"

"Yeah. Lyon gets this cheap shit in Nesconset on Long Island. There's a community of illegals who make this stuff for basically nothing, and we inflate the prices—but it's too hard to explain. So it's settled, then. The mattress is yours."

"Thank you?" I said as if it was a question.

"Thank me later with drinks, girl. Do you need a box spring and a metal frame?"

"I think so."

"You think so? What do you sleep on now?"

"An air mattress."

"Are you kidding me?"

"No."

She started laughing, and I followed suit.

"Oh, Chardonnay, it's good that you came when you came. We're not twenty-one anymore and can't sleep on air mattresses. Let's go upstairs and pick up new sheets as well."

A bell went off above us.

"What's that?" I asked.

"It's the door detector. Means someone's downstairs in the showroom. You go upstairs and see if you like any of the sheets. I'll join you after I'm done with them."

On the third floor, there were dining sets, basic barstools, and kitchen islands, as well as a desk with a computer, and I wondered whether I'd be sitting there soon, answering calls. I sat down on the swivel chair behind the desk and spun around. Then I picked up the phone and played out an imaginary conversation, saying, "Hi, this is Lindsay. Thanks for calling Lyon's. May I help you?"

Giddiness made me smile, and I replaced the receiver.

The fourth floor was half the size of the other three, filled with sheets, draperies, and throw pillows. There was a unisex bathroom, and next to it was a door that said, DO NOT ENTER. STAFF ONLY. I was staff. I tugged on the door, but it was locked.

I rummaged through the sheets until some customers appeared, two bald older men in tracksuits, one of them wearing a gold chain. When I offered them a smile, I received none in return. Once I found the sheets I liked, lavender with a herbarium design, I went downstairs.

By lunchtime, my hangover haze evaporated, elevating my mood. I imagined the reunion with Aspen later that night and could barely wait to see her, a petite brunette who, unlike Cinnamon, typically remained reserved and soft-spoken. She was a year younger than me—Cinnamon was twenty-nine, and Aspen was twenty-five. I realized Aspen was probably going through the quarter-life crisis, seeking answers that nobody seemed to have. Like, what happiness really was, for example.

Cinnamon ordered lunch, two tuna salad sandwiches, which were delivered, and while we ate, we chatted about nothing in particular, somehow avoiding talking about the past. That conversation was reserved for later at Randy's, when drinks would be present.

At fifteen minutes to six, Cinnamon opened the register and pulled out some one-hundred-dollar bills, giving me three.

"And that's how you get paid, girl," Cinnamon said.

"We didn't sell or do anything all day."

"You will, girl. Don't worry. Tuesday are slow—that's all. Something about Tuesdays makes people wanna stay home. It will pick up tomorrow."

Part Three

Randy's

Let me release any grudges, resentments or vendettas against anyone, including myself, that block this radiant heart.

—TOSHA SILVER

Sixteen

At Randy's, Aspen was perched on a stool in a crop top and shorts, both in yellow. A dirty martini stood beside her on a shiny wooden bar top, which ran the bar's length and remained empty of patrons. The bartender, a young redhead, hustled on the other side. The space continued forever and was divided into two sections: dining tables in the front and a gaming section with darts, pool, and cornhole in the back.

The next five minutes was a jambalaya of girls screaming and heads turning. Aspen's brown eyes were outlined with eyeliner and took up half of her face, enormously long, fake lashes touching her brows. Nude lipstick, minimal makeup, and glossy brown hair, straight and put away in a ponytail. She had always been teeny-tiny, but now a little muffin was assembling itself, just like Cinnamon's. Cinnamon ordered a lemon drop martini for herself and said to me, "Pick your poison, girl."

"I'm not sure," I said, questioning my behavior from the night before, unwilling to drink another evening away. "Maybe just some seltzer for me."

"Oh no you don't, girl," she said to me. Then she turned to the bartender and said, "She'll have a cosmopolitan."

When the drinks arrived, the three of us cheered with our respective martini glasses, colored clear, yellow, and pink.

"What a small world," Aspen said mandatorily, using the phrase as connective tissue to the past. "After all these years, three queens returned to Queens, the way the fortune-teller I had in Seattle, Denise, predicted."

"Really?" I asked.

"Yes, she did," Aspen said. "She told me that we'll all three have us some bright futures, irregardless of where we end up. We have them smarts, Denise said. I just can't believe none of ya'll changed, ya'll."

"Aspen, don't be stupid," Cinnamon said. "You can't say *ya'll* twice."

"Why not?"

"Because I said so. You sound like a moron."

"You sound like a complete Sagittarius," I told Aspen.

"I am!" she said.

"See? I knew it," I said.

We giggled and, akin to similar encounters of friends who meet after a lustrum, delved into the past: Remember this? Remember that?

"That just proves that life is short," Aspen said. "Denise said that *infernarents* told her so."

"What the hell are you talking about?" Cinnamon said. "*Infernarents* is not a word."

"Yes, it is. It means, like, heaven or something."

"You mean *firmaments*?"

"That's what I said," Aspen said. "Like, everything ends, Denise said."

"Yes, like your brain," Cinnamon said and laughed.

"I'm saying nothing lasts. What don't you understand? For example, Seattle didn't last for me; Miami didn't last for you; Cookie's club closed."

"What happened to Cookie?" I asked, joining the conversation, only now it was between Cinnamon and me.

"She's at Rikers," she said.

"What's Rikers?"

"A shithole. She's in jail, Chardonnay, on Rikers Island."

"That's insane. I feel so bad for her."

"Don't be surprised, Chardonnay. What did you expect would happen to a dominatrix running an illegal business? I'm surprised she only got a year."

"For what?"

"Illegal gun possession."

"I visited her once," Aspen said. "She has, like, six more months left. Rikers is here in Astoria, but you have to, like, cross the bridge and stuff on a bus. Maybe it's called upstate New York or something. Or Connecticut. I don't know."

"I don't want to waste our evening discussing Cookie," Cinnamon said sternly, and then her voice suddenly changed to sweet and sarcastic. "Aspen, tell us about Seattle. This is a fun story, Chardonnay."

"Seattle was meh," Aspen said and started curling the ends of her hair in a flirtatious way. "But I couldn't care no less about the rain."

"Oh no you don't," Cinnamon said. "His name wasn't *Rain*, ding-dong. That's not why she left. His name was Derick, the guy she moved there for."

"Oh right," Aspen said as if she'd forgotten. "We met here in Astoria—that was after you left, Chardonnay—and moved to Seattle. Well, I moved for him because he got a great position at a tech company. He ended up cheating on me. But I *did* hate the rain."

"What did you expect to happen, Aspen?" Cinnamon said. "You reap what you sow."

"I don't know what that means."

"It means you can get a man out of a strip club, but you can't get the strip club out of the man. Am I right, or am I right? Just like you couldn't get voraciousness out of Cookie, and how you can't get stupidity out of Ichika. It's like dating a guy who just got divorced for cheating and expecting him to be a goody two shoes. Once a cheater, always a cheater. Nobody really changes."

"What's your problem?" Aspen asked. "It's not like he killed me or nothing. That would be bad."

"I don't have a problem," Cinnamon said. "Your personal life is your personal life."

Cinnamon's statement, somehow, appeared the opposite of the truth. Aspen's personal life was now fully Cinnamon's.

Cinnamon told us her story, how she attempted living in Florida for three years, working at various strip clubs around Miami. Competition and rivalry drive profits in Miami. Girls who get hired are tan, incredibly young, and out-of-this-world gorgeous. With a ton of money saved—without specifying the amount—Cinnamon said she'd hopped on a plane and returned to New York before she knew it. She rented a studio in Astoria and started working at a strip club.

"At Cookie's?" I asked.

"I tried," Cinnamon said. "But she didn't hire me. She said I was too old."

"That's why Cinnamon hates Cookie," Aspen said and smiled.

"I don't hate Cookie. I found a job right away without her help. Now I'm at Lyon's, and the two of you are there as well—because of me. Unlike Cookie, I don't hire prepubescent girls who aren't old enough for a driver's license."

This was the second time Cookie was mentioned, and Cinnamon was visibly getting agitated about it. I assumed it was because Cookie denied her the job. In that industry, it's all about rivalry, but perhaps a different conflict was the reason. Cinnamon abruptly stopped her story and turned to me.

"What about you, Chardonnay?" she asked. "How did you end up here? Don't omit a single detail."

Digging up the past takes courage, and for that, a second round of drinks was in order. The bartender spoke with an Irish accent I had a problem understanding, as if something was pushing his tongue up. By this time, a handful of young international guys had appeared alongside the wooden bar, occasionally glancing in our direction.

"I was a live-in nanny," I said. Then lied, "Until the dad attempted having sex with me." I watched Cinnamon's face for support, as if her encouragement was needed for me to proceed.

"Those are rich cocksuckers who live there," Cinnamon said. "Aspen, she makes it sound less than it was. The father of the kids actually tried to rape Chardonnay."

"For real?" Aspen asked.

Lying seemed sweeter, even at the expense of the father. Sometimes, the truth is hard to understand—and by understand, I mean the nuances and all. It's hard for most people to grasp why I quit while following a made-up formula for happiness. I played my "young" and "white privilege" cards, assuming I could find work anywhere. I had a choice of not working at all with the $25,000 I'd saved.

On our third round, the course of the conversation switched to dating. Like me, Aspen and Cinnamon were both single, which is why Randy's had become their favorite watering hole. Single men in their prime frequented, and from our vantage point at the corner in the front, patrons lay open in front of us.

"Check this out, Aspen," Cinnamon said. "Chardonnay had the worst date last night. The guy showed up in freaking flip-flops."

"Sandals," I said.

"Ugh," she said, "even worse."

I wondered how it was worse, but I nodded anyway.

"Disgusting," Cinnamon said, her tongue drunkenly twisting the word. "Look at how beautiful we look. We spend hours getting ready in the morning, starve to death to keep in shape, shave every inch of our bodies, and we're still not making as much money as men, dollar to dollar. And what do guys do? Put on freaking flip-flops. Oops, sorry. I meant sandals. Which is worse. Then girls must give birth, and we can't even get an abortion in every state, especially after the first trimester. That I know for sure. I hate men."

Drunken bottom line, I thought. I learned about that in self-help books. Drunk people always tell the truth.

"Yeah, nothing lasts," Aspen said.

"Including this night," I said. "I must get home."

"No, no, no," Cinnamon begged.

I checked my phone, realizing it was almost 11:00 p.m. There was a missed call and a text message from Lisa. The message was: *"Please replace my kale. Thanks."*

"Guess what my roommate just sent?" I asked. "She said I'd taken her kale, and I didn't touch it. I hate her and her kale."

I wondered whether that was that my bottom line.

"She's an asshole," Cinnamon said. "One more drink and then we go."

Unwilling to deal with reality, also known as Lisa and her kale, I stayed for another drink, which was a big, fat, ugly mistake. For when the morning came and the sunshine beamed through the lacy curtains I'd neglected to draw the night before, I wanted to die. My head hurt in a new, unfamiliar way. Only this time, when my eyes opened, the kleptomaniac was sleeping in my bed, clutching my teddy bear. Like Cinnamon said, "You reap what you sow." Once a kleptomaniac, always a kleptomaniac.

Seventeen

When I awoke to his snoring, I shrieked, and akin to the previous morning, memories flooded. Upon returning home the previous night, I'd texted the misogynist first, but he never replied, so I opted for the next best thing. In my phone, they were saved as *Miso* and *Klepto*.

I quickly scrolled through my text-message spread with Klepto, and heat rushed to my cheeks from embarrassment.

I played no games, it appeared, by texting the kleptomaniac straight up: *"Hi, sexy, what's up? Wanna come over?"*

At 12:30 a.m.

To him, it obviously read as a booty call, and he replied right away. He rang the bell, even after I told him not to, and came up, knocking loudly on the door. If I smelled of alcohol, he smelled of weed, two peas in a pod. He couldn't get "it" up, I recalled, but he wanted to touch me. Right away, without doing any pit stops, his fingers wandered south, avoiding my girl like the plague. I asked what he was doing. He told me to relax, his hand tickling inside my butt cheeks.

"Just stop," I said.

"Why?" he asked.

"I'm not into it."

"It's the only way I like it."

"Then I'm the wrong girl for you," I remembered saying.

"Come on—let's just try it."

I smacked his fingers, but he pushed harder.

"I said no. No means no."

"You say that now, but later you'll beg for it. Just relax."

Somehow, I tackled him off, and he fell on his back, defeated. I skedaddled to the kitchen for a glass of water and to take a breath, and he was fast asleep when I returned. I wanted to kick him out but feared he'd attempt touching me after I told him no. Klepto was an "asshole"—trying to get into mine without my consent.

On our first and only date, he appeared tall, dark, and handsome, but none of those attributes mattered in my bed that morning. What mattered was my stupidity, of which, it seemed, I had tons. His lack of respect for me mirrored my evident lack of respect for myself—nobody with regard for her dignity would invite in someone like him.

While Klepto kept snoring, I grabbed my phone. It was still early morning, 8:30 a.m., and a message from Lisa awaited: *"Could you please be quiet if you bring hookups home so late? Thanks."*

Why couldn't she just leave me alone? Lisa was clearly obsessed with punishing me with her passive-aggressiveness until I apologized for something I didn't do.

My tummy churned, the smell of acid in my mouth. I vigorously tugged on his arm, and he croaked like a frog.

"Hey, get up. You must go," I said, looking in the opposite direction, covering my face with my hair.

"What time is it?" he asked.

"Eight thirty."

"Cool."

He moved behind me, the air mattress wobbling, but I kept staring at the wall in the opposite direction. When he stood up, the air mattress bounced, and I almost fell on my back.

"Get yourself a real mattress," he said. "Jeez Louise."

"I'm planning on it."

"My neck hurts. Massage it over here for me."

Had those words actually come out of his mouth? I looked at him in disbelief, darkness shaping his face into shadows. He sat beside me, took my hand, and placed it on his neck.

"Here," he said.

Between his arrogance and the insult toward my mattress (plus my embarrassment of myself), I dutifully massaged Klepto, tired and hungover, mouth tasting salt from tears. I'd moved to Astoria to avoid just that: humiliation. I had plenty of money to start my life from scratch. What was wrong with me?

Soon he stood up. "You're so bad at it."

"OK," I said quietly.

"I need to book a massage after that horrible night. A hundred bucks, plus tips."

Just like Lisa penalized me with her text messages, Klepto clearly punished me for refusing to surrender last night. When the front door banged, I felt relief that he was out of the apartment, my safe space. As my head kept on pounding, I lay back down, searching for my teddy bear to cuddle. My dignity appeared to have left me somehow, whereas my teddy bear, I realized while searching my bed in the darkness, seemed to have left my apartment. Klepto took it.

I slept until noon, then spent ten minutes returning unanswered text messages, including one from Miso: "*I was asleep last night when you texted me.*"

I ventured out to the kitchen for water, catching a cold glimpse of Lisa, who typed on her computer without saying a word. I showered, dressed, and went to work. I purchased a beef stick wrapped in pita with white sauce from a food cart on the corner and munched while walking in the humid heat.

Eighteen

Ichika had no idea who I was, and she greeted me with a strong accent: "Hi, welcome to Lyon's. Can I help you?"

I spotted Cinnamon on the phone at the desk, dressed in stark red, twice brighter than her auburn hair. I took off my sunglasses, saying, "Hi, are you Ichika? I'm Lindsay, the new hire."

"Oh, Lizzy," she said. "Lyon tell me watch you today. I expect worker, not model, eh? Now Cinnamon is no more prettiest."

"Thank you," I said.

Smiling, Ichika bowed and reached for a hug, but I stepped back, saying, "I'm so sweaty and gross."

"It's OK." And she hugged me anyway.

Cinnamon had mentioned Ichika was sixty, but she looked much younger. Even midforties would be a stretch. She wore horn-rimmed glasses, skin tone fair, sunspots, some lines, and no pores visible. She had black eyes and black hair, which was short, dry, and thinning, pulled away from her face with barrettes clipped at the temples. Ichika was stick-thin, slightly slouchy, and no higher than five foot two. She wore shiny black clogs, blue jeans that I could only imagine were from the kids' department, and a paisley cardigan, her bosom barely noticeable. Cinnamon had been right about sunflower shells being stuck between her teeth.

"First day, eh?" she asked.

"Technically second."

"You live Astoria?"

"Yes, fifteen minutes away from here."

"I'm Flushing. I drive. Quick, quick." As she talked, she pretended to hold a steering wheel in her hands. "You look like model, Lizzy."

"I'm sorry, but it's Lindsay."

"Oh, yes, yes, Lizzy. Let go Cinnamon. She work here. Cinnamon like spice. Funny girl. I like. I introduce. Come."

"I already know Cinnamon and Aspen. We're friends from way back."

"Nice gal. Little lazy, eh? I like anyway. They think they movie star. Always selfie. Pretty, but no boyfriend."

Cinnamon joined us then. Despite being drunker than me last night and while I looked—I could only assume—horrible, Cinnamon glowed. She wore another Leo outfit: red heels and a red power-woman suit with a white tee underneath. Auburn hair, red lipstick, fierce blue eyes. The air conditioner blasted on full, and I regretted forgetting a sweater at home, wearing nothing but a tee, pink skirt, and platform shoes.

"Ichika," Cinnamon said in a sweet, I'm-a-good-girl voice. "Lindsay and I are going to lunch. Could you please watch the front, darling?"

"Good, you is too skinny," Ichika said. "Need eat something."

"You're a doll, Ichika," Cinnamon said.

"Have good lunch. Nice to meet you, Lizzy."

"You too, Ichika," I told her. Then I said to Cinnamon, "I've just come in. Are we really going to lunch?"

"The sooner, the better."

Nineteen

Cinnamon took me to a Mexican restaurant across the street, and upon being seated, I asked her whether I could get in trouble.

"For what?"

"I'm supposed to be working right now."

"It's lunchtime. It's fine."

"You look great today, by the way. Your boobs look huge."

"Thanks, girl. I *feel* amazing. After our reunion last night, I feel incredible. How much fun was that? Just girls, no men. What?"

"Nothing."

"I said *men*; you flinched."

"I didn't flinch, just not feeling well." No way was I telling her about a booty call with Klepto. Last night belonged only to us girls, and I didn't want to spoil the fantasy.

"Hair of the dog," she said and raised her hand, getting the waitress's attention, a curvy Latina with thick black hair.

"Ready to order?" the waitress asked.

"Yes," Cinnamon said. "We'll have two frozen margaritas, mango for me and strawberry for her." Cinnamon waited for my approval, and when I nodded, she continued, "And for lunch, we'll both have fish tacos. Thanks, darling."

Cinnamon returned the menus, showing off her maroon nail polish, and said to me when the waitress left, "Best fish tacos ever. Thank me later."

In the meantime, I debated several related thoughts: How could I possibly eat a second lunch, and will I keep the fish down? How could I possibly drink for the third day in a row? And most importantly, were we allowed to consume alcohol during lunch while on the clock?

Cinnamon detected my uneasiness and said, "Relax, it's totally fine to have a drink with lunch. Chardonnay, you're hilarious. We were trashed at the strip club every night."

"Yes, we were," I said, "but having guys touch you all night long, you better be trashed."

"You don't have to drink, then—no problem," she said. But I sensed it would be a problem if I didn't.

"I want to," I lied. "Maybe that's why I feel uneasy."

"Lyon's on Long Island for a week to deal with his relatives, and Ichika is stupid. Trust me on this. Do you trust me?"

"I trust you," I said, unsure how I actually felt.

Twenty

Cinnamon was correct about one thing: a margarita helped. My anxiety and tiredness associated with the hangover disappeared, leaving me in a woozy state of bliss. Several customers rummaged through the store when we returned. I felt incredibly judgmental, questioning their lack of taste. I wondered whether the judgment stemmed from me judging myself for mistakes and failures in the past two days. According to self-help books I'd devoured in the past few months, it's called *extension*. We extend the judgment about ourselves onto others. Was that true? The thing is, I was exhausted by the seemingly straightforward advice and overly simplistic ideas. So we judge ourselves every time we judge others? Isn't that a bit bizarre? Should we, then, never dislike anything or have negative opinions?

I tailed Cinnamon around the store, getting the gist. The staff (us) could literally be replaced with a cardboard cutout that said, "Yes, we deliver. Same-day delivery is more expensive and depends on the number of orders ahead." No other questions.

I purchased a basic bed frame, the cheapest at the store, for $170, which included my 30 percent employee discount. (The mattress was free.) Cinnamon said it was a good deal while making herself a handsome twenty-five-dollar commission.

Downstairs, Cinnamon introduced me to Juan and Hector, our deliverymen, who were loading the truck for deliveries. My mattress was scheduled to arrive tomorrow from twelve to two. Juan and Hector were tan and Hispanic, with amusingly large mustaches and straw hats.

For whatever reason, Klepto appeared in my head. He talked shit about my air mattress after I disallowed him to enter my back door. I shook the image when Cinnamon tugged on my skirt.

"Girl, look," she said.

"What am I looking at?"

"Ichika eating her lunch."

Ichika was leisurely spread on a leather armchair with a bowl of instant noodles on her lap. She enthusiastically slurped on the long strands, recovering them from the bowl with chopsticks.

"So what?" I said.

"No manners."

"Oh."

"So much sodium too. That's why she has those huge puffs under her eyes."

"What kind of cancer does she have?"

"Sure, Chardonnay. We can talk about that too. She used to have it—breast. And then she removed them, which is why she's so flat."

Ten minutes later, while Cinnamon taught me how to fill out delivery orders, a young couple walked in, talking inaudibly, her holding an iced coffee with milk, him carrying her purse. She wore a sports bra and biker shorts, and he wore a tank top and shorts that stopped midthigh, revealing hairy legs.

"What do you think of them?" Cinnamon asked.

"What do I think of them?"

"Yes."

"Well," I said. "He's obviously a hairy beaver."

"No, silly. Why are they here?"

"Beats me. I'm not Aspen's psychic, Denise."

"Watch and learn," she said. "Look at the frump. She's preggo, maybe five months."

"Oh," I said, noticing the belly with a protruding belly button.

"So they need furniture but probably on a budget anyway. They're in business for an inexpensive crib, but they may also want more new stuff with the new baby coming in. They're on that 'everything is new' kind of phase. Which, they don't know, will end as soon as the baby arrives. I feel so bad for them. Come on—let's make a sale."

Cinnamon approached them with, "Hi, darlings, I'm Cinnamon. Can I help you find anything?"

"We're just browsing around," the woman said. "Nothing specific."

By nothing specific, she meant three-grand worth of furniture that Cinnamon sold them in the next thirty minutes: a crib, a brown leather couch (suitable for spills with the new baby), and a new bed for mommy and daddy. Same-day delivery would be a hundred bucks, but

Cinnamon said she'd waive it for them, which prompted the woman to add a leather armchair, four pillows, and sheets. A thousand dollars later … The commission for that sale, I calculated, was $400. Once the man swiped his credit card and the card reader beeped approvingly, I understood why Cinnamon loved the job. She took four Benjamins out of the cash register, saying, "That's how you cash out your commission."

As I remembered from our days at the strip club, Cinnamon was as madly in love with cash as I was. I played a pretend conversation in my head, in which I confronted Cinnamon about the easiness of the job. This is what I envisioned:

"Easy, bitch?" she'd say. "You think sleeping in curlers is easy? You think Botox, masks, and hair extensions are easy? You think waking up at the crack of dawn is easy? You think spending hours in front of a mirror blending makeup is easy? You think matching outfits is easy?"

"Chardonnay, what's up?" Cinnamon asked me, squeezing my shoulder.

I realized I'd been zoning in and out of sleep on the desk chair after the sale. The hangover, two lunches, and frozen margarita took a toll on my body.

"I'm fine," I said.

"Great. We're leaving."

"What time is it?"

"Fifteen minutes to five."

"I think I'm supposed to stay with Ichika until eight."

"Forget Ichika. When Lyon leaves town, he leaves her in charge, and she's at work all day from open to close like a slave. So let her close by herself."

"So stalwart of her."

"Girl, please. She's just stupid. Here's your pay for today."

Cinnamon handed me three Benjamins. Combined with the money from yesterday, my rent was paid—by doing nothing. I picked up the cash unwillingly, as if I were stealing it.

"Follow me," Cinnamon said.

I rubbed my eyes and grabbed my purse, putting the money inside.

We approached Ichika, who was talking to a customer, an older Indian woman in a colorful, beautiful sari, a bindi on her forehead. Compared to the woman, monotone Ichika faded into the background of ugly brown leather furniture.

"Ichika, darling," Cinnamon interrupted, "we're leaving for the day. Then Lindsay and I are off for the weekend, and Aspen closes tomorrow." Then she whispered to me, "Let's go."

"Bye-bye," Ichika said and bowed. "See you."

Outside, I said, "That's it, my whole day? And then two days off on top?"

"Do you finally understand why I love this job? Let's go—Aspen's waiting at Randy's."

"We're going to Randy's?"

"Naturally."

"Is Aspen's legal name also Aspen?"

"No, she uses a nickname, but she's thinking about changing it legally. The name Aspen suits her, don't you agree?"

"Why do you say that?"

"Aspen is a ski-resort town, and that girl is all about skiing. Do you know what I'm saying?"

"No."

"Skiing up her nose."

Cinnamon laughed and, awkwardly, I followed suit.

Twenty-One

Randy's was empty and quiet when we entered at five. Aside from the three of us, two guys had a soundless conversation in a corner by the window. The waiter and the bartender from the previous night, both young Irish men, worked on getting the bar set up. My skin felt on fire after a fifteen-minute walk in the scorching heat, swamp ass and all.

Looking around the empty, massive bar, I briefly wondered how the rent at Randy's got paid without any patrons. Other bars along Thirtieth Avenue crawled with people. The formula was as follows: the closer to the subway, the more crowded the bar. Since I lived five blocks away from the subway, the bars nearby always seemed jammed with patrons—including that hip bar on Thirty-Fourth Street where I almost had a date with James, the guy in sandals. As street numbers increased, the number of people in bars proportionally diminished. Randy's stood on a lone corner of Forty-Fourth Street, basically in the middle of nowhere, far away from the subway, grocery stores, and gyms. Walking one extra block in this excessive heat meant life and death, humidity unbearable and quite literally life-threatening.

Cinnamon, however, barely perspired, and her white V-neck looked only slightly damp under her arms.

"I'm dying from the humidity," I said and hugged Aspen, who looked like a Barbie doll in a ponytail and a beige tank top, revealing bronze, glowing shoulders.

"Aren't you from Florida?" Aspen asked.

"Yes, so?"

"Well, it's humid there," she said. "You should be used to it by now."

"Aspen, don't be stupid," Cinnamon said. "If you grew up in poverty, it doesn't mean you get used to it, and if you grew up in Florida, it doesn't mean your body magically stops perspiring."

"What are you talking about?" Aspen said. "You said so yourself yesterday. Chardonnay, back me up here. She said people never change."

"I meant *emotionally* people don't change," Cinnamon said, fanning her face with her hand. "But they change physically. I need to dive into a bucket of ice. This suit was a bad idea."

She raised her hand, calling the waiter over. "Three martinis, please. A dirty with three olives, a lemon drop, and a cosmopolitan. We're classy bitches."

My plan to avoid alcohol, therefore, failed miserably. With Cinnamon in charge, nobody seemed to protest, and drinks flowed freely. That evening at Randy's, Aspen mimicked Cinnamon the way Lise mimicked Lisa. Same language and gesticulations. They seemed to understand each other on a deeper, subconscious level, and when one talked, the other listened without interruption. Such a realization was sudden, like a bolt of lightning. In each pair, one girl appeared the leader while the other one was the follower: the yin and the yang. When my roommates argued, compromise followed when the weaker one, Lise, the perpetual Virgo, eventually gave in, finding fights unbearable and unnecessary. Aspen, a Sagittarius, never seemed to win any battles either.

I don't recall coming home. Thankfully, upon getting up, no man was found on my air mattress.

Twenty-Two

At noon, Juan and Hector delivered my mattress. They assembled a metal bed frame, placed a generic box spring, and finished with the mattress like a cherry on top. The bed soared high above my hip. When they finished, I tipped them twenty bucks each, and soon they left, the most effortless delivery of my life. I made the bed with my newly purchased lavender sheets. Then I deflated the air mattress and put it in Lise's room next to her armoire.

I unwillingly ventured to the living room, afraid to run into Lisa, but her bedroom door stood open. Liam had a share on Fire Island for a week, and Lise was still at the realtor conference in Washington, DC. I wondered where Lisa was if not at home. As far as I knew, she didn't have any friends aside from Lise. Why would she have any friends, with that Scorpio personality of hers? I still hadn't spoken to her two days later and didn't mind the break from that coldhearted, analytical accountant. Right now, the last thing I needed was to get upset about the missing kale, which was probably juiced by the forgetful, absent-minded Lise. Seriously, kale costs two bucks. If she needed it that badly, she should have gone and bought it. Which proved Lisa didn't need it. It was the principle of the thing for her. Which proved she was a bitch.

Cinnamon texted, "*What are you doing tonight?*"

"Not sure. Why?"

"Randy's?"

"Sure."

"I'll pick you up on the way at seven."

I opted for a quick, five-mile run, then showered and dressed. Polka-dotted mini dress in pastel green and heels. I love running because it makes you sweat, and that removes any facial bloating and excess salt. Plus, my calves were looking great. I lathered myself in sparkling lotion, admiring my tan skin and blonde waves. Ichika was right: I resembled a model.

While walking to Randy's with Cinnamon, I found it interesting that I kept mixing Randy's the bar with Rikers the jail, and whenever Cinnamon mentioned Randy's, an image of Cookie wearing orange popped in. I was fortunate to have departed the strip-club industry, or I might have ended up at Rikers with Cookie.

I shared my thoughts with Cinnamon. "Don't you think *Randy's* and *Rikers* sound similar?"

She seemed dismissive about it. "Don't be ridiculous, Chardonnay. It's like saying two fat girls look alike because they're overweight."

"Interesting analogy."

"Do you remember how I made that Irish guy pay for our drinks last night?"

I was thrown off by the non sequitur. "No."

"Do you want me to teach you how it's done?"

"Why? It's only a couple of drinks. I can afford it."

"Men are supposed to pay for us, Chardonnay. After everything we've endured for them in strip clubs, they owe us big time."

I wondered why Cinnamon sounded bitter about it. "So is it a payback?"

"Payback barely begins to cover it. I won't stop until all of them suffer—emotionally, physically, and financially. Given the chance, I'd personally castrate all the motherfuckers. They can show up in sandals or with their dicks hanging out, and yet, we're the ones getting paid less and giving birth to these assholes. Do you know they used to kill baby girls in China? They probably still do."

"No. Why would they?"

"Because they considered girls unimportant. It's all about them. Chardonnay, it's good we met when we met because you and Aspen have experienced the humiliation firsthand, and you both understand what I'm talking about. Remember how they pawed you during lap dances? Don't you want to travel back in time and punch them in the face?"

"I never thought of it that way," I lied, because I had.

There was a reason I'd read a million self-help books, trying to fill a void inside me. I'd been a cliché my entire life, following what every girl in my position had done. After the foster-parent system, you drop out of high school and start working at a strip club to make a living, then you get involved with some douchebag in a tracksuit and end up rotting in jail at Rikers like Cookie.

Just two days prior, I felt elated, like I was finally getting to the surface of it all—like I understood happiness. Cinnamon showed me that I'd been lying to myself by trying to patch the wound without healing it first. Now I felt anger, at nobody in particular. Just anger. For years, I thought that once I found happiness—real, end-of-a-movie kind of happiness—I'd never have any negative emotions. But I had plenty. Was happiness an illusion?

In the past, yoga and meditation helped me, to an extent. But when memories of the past resurfaced and I experienced PTSD, insomnia, breakouts, and psoriasis. Happiness, yet again, slipped away, vague and unattainable. I kept running after it, naive enough to believe I would eventually find it. And whenever I believed I reached my final destination—a state of bliss—I inevitably clung to it for dear life, but then it disappeared into the darkness. Was it all a mirage?

These were my thoughts on the way to Randy's, realizations that made me think that the fourth cornerstone of happiness—a relationship with a man—had been incorrect the entire time. I felt content with Cinnamon, a woman, but with men, it had always felt complicated. Cinnamon had been through what I'd been through. She related to me.

I understood now.

It was like euphoria! We read self-help books, and while one solution works for one person, it fails to work for another. Why is that? I knew exactly why. Because we all live on different planets. Not just men on Mars and women on Venus. Each of us lives on entirely different planets, distant from one another, unrelatable. We simply can't convert the pain experience from one person to the next because what hurts you won't necessarily hurt me.

But Cinnamon and I lived on the same planet, and she understood on a deeper level. She helped me find a good-paying, easy job where I don't pay taxes. And now she wanted to teach me how to save money by not paying for my drinks. Therefore, the fourth cornerstone of happiness was about building a relationship with someone from a similar background—not a man or a woman. Anyone. That's why, I realized, I'd been so unhappy. Because when my stripper friends moved away, I became friends with Candace, who talks about nothing but vaginas and whose happiness is conditional. Then with that privileged, pessimistic Aquarius Chloe, who only knows how to complain because she's lazy and hates herself. And then with Nikita, whose optimism pulls the wool over her eyes.

But now two of my friends had returned, and we became inseparable. Because we understood each other's pain. Despite how smart or mature Lisa and Lise were, they could never understand my story. Their "grown-up" advice, whenever they gave me any, suddenly seemed childish and unimportant because it wasn't conveyed through Cinnamon's filter.

That evening, when Cinnamon opened the door to Randy's, I felt elated. I felt like I grew up a thousand years, for I finally understood the importance of a new cornerstone. The support system.

Here were my new cornerstones of happiness:

Healthy body
Independence
Important vocation
Support system

Twenty-Three

The next day, Cinnamon called me in the morning. We chatted briefly about how much fun the previous night was. Thankfully, nothing happened, and I controlled my alcohol intake. We did manage to make an Irish guy pay for all our drinks, though, which was the goal. When Aspen showed up after work, we played pool while going down memory lane.

And at the end of our conversation, Cinnamon said, "I'll come over at three to pick you up."

"Where are we going?"

"Shopping. Too-da-loo," she said, then hung up.

Cinnamon buzzed in at ten minutes to three. She wore a frill-trim cami top in baby blue, which accentuated her blue eyes, contrasting with tan skin and auburn hair, which she wore down. She had on platforms and white pants.

"Cinnamon, you look amazing!"

"Thanks, darling, so do you," she said, giving me a kiss on the cheek, then walking in. "Is the old bag home?" she whispered.

"Who?"

"Lisa."

"No."

"Great. Let me see your new mattress. Where's your bedroom?"

While in my room, Cinnamon said, "I love the sheets you picked out. And love the dresser too. Gorge."

She opened the top drawer while I yelled, "Cinnamon!"

"Oh, relax," she said. "I just wanted to see your panties." She started giggling like a little girl and shut the drawer.

Before we exited the apartment, Cinnamon paused to put on a fake belly around her waist.

"Oh my God," I said. "You still do that fake baby bump?"

"Of course."

Memories of the past flooded. "You're the only girl I know who's been pregnant for the past five years."

"Hey, if it works, it works. I realized the bump is no longer for getting a seat on a crowded subway. For example, waiters give me free stuff all the time. I get special treatment while flying, even upgrades to first class."

"Really?"

"Trust me—I've talked myself out of tickets in Florida, like, a hundred times. You should get a bump for yourself. In fact, I'll get it for your birthday. When's that?"

"April first," I said.

"I'll give it to you for Labor Day, then, because it's sooner."

"How fitting," I said. "Baby bump for Labor Day. Labor," I repeated, and we burst out laughing until we both were teary.

"Oh my God, Chardonnay, you better stop. I'm dying."

"Do you still shoplift with this thing?"

"What do you think, bitch? My commission at the store is not for buying clothes."

"Then what?"

"I'm saving for my retirement, but the girl still has to look her best."

"You're already retiring?"

"Girl, I'm not a dumbass Ichika, OK? I won't be sixty-odd years old working under an idiot, and I won't end up like my crazy mom, rotting in a prison in Florida. Once I get enough cash, I'm moving to Key West, where the beach and mojitos are within reach. Aspen wants in too. Are you coming with us, Chardonnay?"

"Beach and mojitos? I'm there!"

Part Four

Lyon's

The quality, not the longevity, of one's life is what is important.

—MARTIN LUTHER KING, JR.

Twenty-Four

I left for work at eight thirty the next day, grabbing an iced coffee on the way. The cool summer breeze swept through, bringing in the aroma of the fresh, salty ocean. My happiness was palpable, the kind of bliss I'd unsuccessfully tried to achieve with self-help books. But none of them mentioned that once I met Cinnamon, my life would change from zero to a hundred—in the best of ways.

I believe that gravity isn't only for space objects and science. Gravity is also true for relationships. Someone like Cinnamon, a Leo (a sun sign), attracted people with incredible force, and we all followed her. The fact that we'd found each other again proves my point. It doesn't matter if we move away, for somehow, somewhere, we'd be attracted to each other's gravitational force.

Why I went all scientific all of a sudden was funny, so I giggled as I walked. I wore a wide-brimmed hat and a polka-dotted sundress that Cinnamon had shoplifted for me the day before. (If I had paid for it, I'd have shelled out $450, by the way.) I carried a sweater in my bag to brace the brutal air conditioner at work. Young professionals hurried robotically toward the subway while garbage trucks went up and down one-way streets. Cinnamon texted me in the morning, saying she'd be late because she had tooth cleaning at nine.

As I walked in, Ichika waved from the back of the store, and I waved as well. She resembled a bee in a yellow tee with black stripes, under a yellow sweater, with black pants that outlined her stick legs. When I approached the desk where she stood, Ichika smiled and bowed.

"*Konnichiwa*, Lizzy. Good to see you," she sang. The ending of each sentence sounded like a question.

"What's that word?"

"'Hello' in Japanese. *Konnichiwa*."

"*Konnichiwa*," I repeated like a monkey. "I never learned another language in school, not even Spanish. I'm a little jealous that you can speak two."

"I speak English, Japanese, and German. I teach you Japanese now, OK? Ready? *Ichi* mean 'one.' *Ni*, like on your leg, mean 'two.' *San*, like sun in sky, mean 'three.'"

"*Ichi, ni, san*," I said.

"So easy, Lizzy." The rhyme made her laugh, and she closed her mouth with her palm, her black eyes shining with energy.

"How do you say *four* in Japanese?"

She immediately stopped laughing. "We no have number four in Japan. Unlucky number, Lizzy."

"You still have it, though, don't you?"

"Four mean death in Japan. We have two word—*shi* and *yon*. *Shi* mean 'death' but also mean 'four.' You say *yon*, which also mean 'four.' But we rather no say four. One, two, three, five. No four."

Was that a bunch of gibberish, or did I understand that they don't have the number four in Japan? I wondered how inconvenient it must be, as the Fourth of July was just next month. I briefly thought that the four cornerstones of happiness in Japan would have to be diminished to three, and I chuckled at my own silliness. Cornerstones and gravity. I was all over the place today.

What about the Japanese calendar? Do the Japanese people skip day four every month? *Ichi*, *ni*, and *san*. Except for *ichi* today was what you'd call my skin—my new dress irritated me, making me literally itch.

When the phone rang, Ichika picked up while I texted Cinnamon: *"Ichika is teaching me Japanese."*

"Oh Lord. Did she go through the whole thing that there's no number four in Japan?"

"Just did."

"That's why Ichika thinks we never could get a fourth person to work at the store. Someone either steals money or leaves without any notice. Ichika says it's because we need to have a fifth person or just have three. But three is too few, and five is too many."

"Oh my God. So superstitious."

"She is."

"Get your ass over here."

"In ichi hours, Chardonnay."

Twenty-Five

The rest of the day went by uneventfully. I set up a couple of deliveries, but Cinnamon was in charge and cashed out my commission. At noon, Aspen joined us for lunch across the street, and we made plans to go to the beach on the Fourth of July when the store was closed.

At home, Lisa and Lise chatted in the living room, TV on mute but playing in the background. I went to the kitchen to say hi to Lise and unload groceries that I'd picked up on the way. Since the kitchen overlooked the living room, the two turned in my direction. Whereas Lise's eyes lit up in a friendly manner, Lisa's icy demeanor matched the blasting air conditioner. Lise stood up from the couch and reached for a hug. Lisa remained seated with a pillow in her lap, which she petted as if it were a cat. Lise had just arrived and wore work clothes, a mustard blazer with matching pants and a scarf.

"How was DC?" I asked as she hugged me.

"It was boring," she said. "I hate DC because it's not a town but a snoozefest. Seriously, there are more circles all over the city than people. Renting a car was a bad idea. But I went shopping in Georgetown and bought you a souvenir."

Lise dashed into the living room and returned with a coin purse with the Washington Monument stitched in white on green fabric representing the National Mall. I felt something round inside the purse.

"Lise, it's adorable."

"Do you like it?"

"I love it. What's inside?"

"Open it."

I unzipped the purse and dipped my fingers inside, where I found a nut of some sort.

"What's this?" I asked.

"A nutmeg."

"That's a nutmeg?" I asked as if she hadn't just told me that. "I never knew what a nutmeg looks like." It was quite ordinary, grayish-brown, wrinkly. "Why did you put it there?"

"During the conference, I met this psychic, who told me, quote, 'You have this aura about you. Like, you have a roommate who needs protection. She's young, blonde, light eyes.' Unquote."

"Me?"

"I know it sounds crazy. But she's like, 'Give her a whole nutmeg and have her carry it with her. Nutmeg will protect her.'"

"Carry it around like a talisman?"

"Why not? It's tiny. Just drop it somewhere in your bag and forget about it."

"OK, thank you."

"Do you like your new job?" she asked.

"I love it so far. Ichika taught me some Japanese today, and Cinnamon showed me how to price-check in our computer system."

"Sounds interesting."

"Not bad."

"Hey, Lisa," Lise said and turned toward the living room, "didn't you want to say something to Lindsay?"

Lisa stood up, throwing the pillow she held back on the couch. I squeezed the nutmeg in my palm, trying to extract power from it, if it had any available, that was. Lisa approached the kitchen and rested her back against the refrigerator, folding her arms.

"I feel bad about what happened," Lisa said, then looked at Lise, as if needing her approval. Lise nodded, so Lisa continued, "I didn't mean to say your pictures were fake. I was incredibly upset about not having any matches and lashed out at you, which was unfair. I'm sorry."

Suddenly, a million pounds dropped from my shoulders, scattering into thin air. The abhorrence I felt for her up until that moment had dissipated in seconds after she apologized. How can that one word—*sorry*—be the hardest thing to say and yet also be so liberating?

"That's OK," I said, then smiled. "I didn't mean it when I called you a liar either. I was just hurt."

"Oh, thank God," Lise said, smiling. "I knew the two of you would make up. Now, about the kale. I'm sorry, but it's all on me."

That evening, Cinnamon called me at ten as I climbed into bed with a self-help book about leadership.

"Hello," I said.

"Hello," Aspen sang.

"Aspen?" I asked. "I thought Cinnamon called me."

"It's a three-way," Cinnamon said. "Welcome to the future, Chardonnay. I'm literally having a glass of chardonnay, by the way. So I'm technically drinking you."

"So scandalous," Aspen said. "We should record our conversations and sell them to some pervert."

"Like the kleptomaniac," Cinnamon said. "Chardonnay, did you tell Aspen about that asshole?"

"No," I said.

"What happened?" Aspen asked.

"I went on a date with a kleptomaniac who's only into anal."

"For real?" Aspen said. "Did he try to . . . you know?"

"What?" I asked. "Get in my ass? Absolutely. I told him no, but he kept on pushing."

"I'll murder him," Cinnamon said. "He basically tried to rape her, Aspen."

"What a pervert!" Aspen said.

"All men are perverts," Cinnamon said. "Am I right, or am I right?"

Twenty-Seven

I curled up under the sheets with my book, but my mind wandered toward happiness. Chloe had never seemed happy, and it made sense that out of the four cornerstones, she had zero. She had money—that's it. So clearly, financial situation meant nothing when happiness was concerned. Chloe was overweight and therefore unhealthy. She lived with her mom and consequently was dependent on homecooked meals and a cleaning lady. She couldn't get a job because of her laziness, and she had no support system. Alcoholics and drug users go to meetings, people with cancer go on cancer walks, and even autism gets plenty of publicity. Why, then, couldn't she admit she was lonely and do something about it?

As I learned from self-help books, we project our anger on other people. Chloe and Lisa hated themselves, for they projected their anger on me. At least Lisa acknowledged and apologized. Would Chloe become happy once she got a job, or would that happiness dissolve the following week when something went wrong?

My transgender friend Candace seemed angry about living in the wrong body, and her happiness appeared to be conditional. She believed becoming a woman would suddenly turn her into someone else, giving her special powers. Self-help books teach us that love comes from within, and it doesn't matter what we look like: fat or thin, ugly or pretty, black or white. We need to find that happiness within, regardless of our looks.

I firmly believed in the cornerstones of happiness, but clearly, neither Chloe nor Candace wanted to take my advice. And what the hell? If they wanted to be unhappy for the rest of their lives, it was their choice.

Nikita was the opposite and was too happy, becoming oblivious about her situation. She was getting married in September, and I knew that once Joaquin received his citizenship in three years, he'd dump her. And Nikita would move on to someone else, repeating patterns. I learned from self-help books that we repeat patterns because they're familiar, even if that means sacrificing our happiness. We remain in abusive relationships because they remind us of our past, regardless of how terrible that past might have been.

Days and weeks were passing by, and each day working at Lyon's, I became more connected—sororal, even—to Aspen and Cinnamon but somehow, proportionally, disconnected from the rest of the world. I used social media less because now, suddenly, I had what other people tried to create—a life.

If the cornerstones of happiness were building blocks, then there were the cornerstones of unhappiness, too, destructive blocks. Boredom was one of them. The world was a balance, the yin and the yang, positivity and negativity. I'd been unhappy in the past, but now I felt the opposite. Aside from gaining the four cornerstones of happiness, the negative four proportionally dissipated:

1. Boredom. I was finally happy I had a life that I enjoyed. I was not a stripper at Cookie's strip club, nor was I a nanny. I was a salesperson, a vital part of our team. My evenings were spent with friends who didn't always complain about something (like Chloe) or want to talk about vaginas (like Candace). Most important, they were available, unlike Nikita.

2. I stopped clinging to my emotional pain. I learned that people cling to negative emotions because it helps them stay in control (like Chloe). When everything goes awry and you end up homeless, for example, at least you have cancer, and it's yours, and nobody can take it away from you. Believe it or not, for many people, clinging to their pain helps them survive. But pain is pain. It's yours, sure, but at what cost?

3. Dating was no longer the answer to self-fulfillment. I deleted dating apps because meeting guys at Randy's was more fun. This was real life on Earth, not on some backed-up cloud. Which is how I realized I no longer had the most destructive termite that slowly chewed on the foundation of happiness, number four on the list.

4. I stopped relying on social media. My social interactions had become real—in person. I met dozens of customers daily, and we laughed and chatted, and those interactions were in person. But Lisa remained by her window without talking to a soul, becoming bitter and

dissatisfied with her life. All of them (including Chloe, Candace, and Nikita) lived online in virtual reality. I no longer wanted to be on social media, not even for a second, and even despised it.

Part Five

Asbury Park

The hard thing about death is that nothing ever changes. The hard thing about life is that nothing stays the same.

—SUE GRAFTON

Twenty-Eight

It was one phone call, too essential to be a text message. From the family for whom I'd worked as a nanny. I found it random to see the mother's name, Lucy Brownstein, calling me. Her contact photo was her holding the youngest daughter, Charlotte. I knew right away that the news couldn't be good, but it was even worse when I picked up.

Twenty-Nine

"Kitty . . . died?" Cinnamon said, unable to believe it.

I placed the phone to my other ear, my heart fluttering. "Shot by a cop."

The room was spinning, and I thought I was suffocating.

"Chardonnay, are you OK?"

"I just can't believe it. She was twenty-nine."

"Do you want me to come over?"

"Let's meet at Randy's."

And we did.

I believe in karma, and I also believe that negative words hold power. When we wish for something to happen, it eventually will—a day or thirty years from now. That's the law of attraction. The universe must rearrange a few things for your wish to come true.

Chloe's hatred for Kitty made that happen. Because thoughts are powerful, especially unkind, detestable ones.

Now I wished Chloe were dead. I wasn't sure how much I meant it, but I meant it on some level.

On the day of the funeral, somewhere along the way to the Bronx, I think I lost a piece of me on the 4 Train. I felt a void I'd never experienced before. Kitty and I hadn't even been that close! *Why* was I so upset?

I was mad at Chloe for making this happen, and I was mad at Kitty for leaving us. I was mad that it was bright and sunny outside because, in movies, it rains during funerals. I wanted rain and gloom. I hated the sun because it reminded me that life was happening everywhere else and people were happy.

"I've never felt such sadness," I said.

"I'm sure you have," Cinnamon said. "Your mother left you at a hospital."

"We weren't even that close. I feel responsible for her death somehow."

"You're not responsible, Chardonnay. You're sad because Kitty was a good girl. You're sad that someone like her, gorgeous and full of potential, died so young. You're sad knowing if she were white, the funeral might not have happened."

"Kitty has two kids, and she helped her mom financially. With rent, bills, everything. How will they deal with that?"

"Tough."

"I don't feel like myself, Cinnamon. It's a bizarre feeling, as if I'm detaching from myself, peeling layers of my personality off like an onion."

"What you're feeling is grief, Chardonnay. It's normal to feel sad and angry when somebody leaves you."

"I felt the same way when you moved to Florida five years ago without saying goodbye."

"Don't compare the two situations—this one is permanent. I've had an amazing life. But you lost a friend forever, and when you lose a friend, even not a close one, you lose a friendship with it. You never know how you'll react. Death shows, in one brusque moment, that life is finite."

"What I'm feeling is not sadness or anger. It's a void, a sort of vacuum."

Cinnamon took my hand into hers. "We will get through this together."

"I know this will sound crazy, but an acquaintance of mine was once livid that Kitty took the nanny job, and I think she wished her dead."

"Like voodoo?"

"No, just the power of thoughts."

"You *do* sound crazy, Chardonnay."

"Chloe is the crazy one. She wished to have that job, loathing Kitty and me. She yelled at me that I hadn't offered it to her."

"Well, fuck Chloe. Cut her out of your life."

"I don't wanna cut anyone out. I want to cut her *up*, Cinnamon. That's the problem. When Lucy called me, she asked if I knew someone who could be a replacement."

"What? The crone seriously asked you that?"

"No joke. The night she called ... like the third sentence out of her mouth."

"People are ridiculous. Why don't you suggest that Chloe girl and let Lucy deal with that psychotic cunt?"

"Chloe is mentally unstable and clearly is a witch of some kind. I care about the children."

"Oh, Chardonnay. Don't get into conspiracy theories. Life is unpredictable, and you're not responsible for finding a replacement—or for Kitty's life or Chloe's job. It's all coincidental."

"I told Lucy I didn't know anyone."

"That's the spirit, Chardonnay. That's called payback, and that Chloe girl better know about it."

"I don't know if I can ever be happy again."

"You will be. Take this." Cinnamon fumbled in her purse and placed a pill in my palm.

"What's this?"

"Just trust me."

Being numb is better than feeling emotional. The funeral passed before my eyes, and I felt no sadness or happiness. I was in a gray area in between, devoid of compassion and anger.

There are five stages of grief: denial, anger, bargaining, depression, and acceptance. Before Cinnamon's pill, I was in stage one: denial. I had no idea how I could possibly get to the last stage. But pill after pill helped me numb the pain, and I didn't even want to know what they were.

When a week flew by and I finished the pills, I realized my body craved more.

"I gave you thirty prescription opioids," Cinnamon said at Randy's the next Friday. "You polished them off in a week? Girl."

"I need more and something more substantial."

"If you want something more substantial, I'll give you something more substantial. But don't go crazy on opioids."

"What are you gonna give me?"

"A fun white powder."

Aspen said, "She means Molly."

"What's Molly?" I asked.

"It's like ecstasy," Aspen said. "It makes you fall in love with everyone."

"It sounds good," I said. "I need that."

"We shouldn't push her, Aspen. Chardonnay, when you *really* feel down, Molly could actually be a fun thing for the three of us to do. For now, try some coke."

"You have coke on you?" I asked.

Cinnamon raised her brows. "What do you think, Chardonnay? There's no other way to live."

We went to the ladies' room, where Cinnamon created three lines, which we dutifully sniffed with a rolled-up bill. The coke numbed my nose, a strange feeling that carried on to the rest of my body. Within minutes, any tiredness and hunger dissipated. I became lighter and lighter until I felt like a cloud, like I could fly. I quickly understood why people got addicted to coke … because the white stuff was a miracle in powdered form.

Thirty-One

It was now late June, and every day had been the same so far: hot, humid, and sunny—hadn't rained once. Days at Lyon's were followed by evenings at Randy's like clockwork. While I felt exhausted physically, I felt optimistic emotionally—a reversal. I loved feeling tired in the morning because it meant I'd had a great time the night before with the girls, even if most mornings I barely remembered anything. Twice I brought home a guy I'd met that night, and twice I texted the misogynist, who preferred me inebriated because he was most often inebriated himself. Our sexual encounters were indistinct in my mind, and I blame the alchemy for that. Actually, I don't blame anything. I drank because I *wanted* to forget my sexual encounters and a weird void that started with Kitty's death. Right before that, I'd felt intense happiness, and now nothing seemed to matter but drugs and alcohol. My conception of happiness, therefore, might have been an illusion.

I rarely saw Lyon at the store. When I did see him, he seemed odd, off, gone even. Several times—I'm pretty sure drugs were involved—he came and behaved nothing like a boss or somebody in change. His swollen, bloodshot eyes would dart in every direction, pupils dilated, capillaries red. Cinnamon would grab him and spend an hour in his office with him. One time I sneaked upstairs and listened outside the locked door, and I could swear he was moaning—crying, I thought—as if Cinnamon was his unofficial therapist. She'd been mine when Kitty passed. The first time it happened, I pretended like Lyon was the last thing on my mind and asked Cinnamon in between tasks, "What was that about? Is he OK?"

"He's fine."

No explanation since.

If he'd been crying to Cinnamon about something, it was strange that a man in his position—with money, a wife, a family, and his own business (with all the cornerstones, if such existed)—would be upset. If Lyon was unhappy, what did it mean for the rest of the poor, unprivileged, underpaid men and women? Were we doomed?

I avoided thinking about it.

Outside of work, the three of us rented cars and drove to the beach, sometimes for a couple of hours before work, and my skin looked golden and delicious. The sun further bleached my hair, and I loved the effect it had on my eyes. They appeared deeper in color, alternating between gray and green. And everything looked good with that combination, especially a bikini.

We were tanning at the beach when Cinnamon said, "Imagine living your life on Key West, ladies. Beach, every day. You walk out of your condo, and the water is right there. One day, we will all move there. I promise. First, we save our money, and off we go, free as birds. As long as none of us does something stupid, like get into a relationship or make babies."

"I don't need babies," I said, tipsy on mojitos and high on coke. "I'll just borrow your fake baby bump if I'm feeling maternal."

"I hope to have them babies one day," Aspen said.

"You're a baby yourself, Aspen," Cinnamon said.

"That's what Cookie calls me too. A baby," Aspen said, which made Cinnamon mad.

"Stop bringing up Cookie. She exploited us, Aspen, and if she wasn't in jail, you would probably still work there. Pawed like a possession of hers."

"You're right," Aspen said.

I noticed that Aspen always agreed with Cinnamon in the end. Cookie and Cinnamon had a similar personality, and Aspen was being passed around like a ball in between, trying to choose a side.

Aspen is the type of person who goes with the flow and needs a strong leader like Cinnamon to operate in life. Whatever Cinnamon says, Aspen follows. I wondered if that was a sign of weakness or a sign of respect. After all, some of us need leaders in our lives, whereas others need followers. I wasn't sure where I was on the spectrum because sometimes I felt like leading and other times like following. When I was at work with Cinnamon, she was in charge, but I was the boss with Aspen when Cinnamon was absent.

It was now July second, and I was at Lyon's with Aspen and Ichika. Aspen wore a crane-print dress in pink, highlighting her protruding collarbones. I looked at her all day, thinking that clearly, Lyon had a type when it came to labor, for the three of us could have been sisters if noted by an impartial observer. I know for a fact that 80 percent of men have a sister-related sexual fantasy, and Lyon, perhaps, was one of them.

Today, even if Cinnamon was off, she basically worked in spirit as she kept texting me silly questions every few minutes.

She'd text: "*Chardonnay, why you can't put a housewife on a stripper pole?*"

"*Why?*"

"*That question is hard, but while the housewife is up there on the pole, nobody else will be hard.*"

I sent her a laughing emoji back. "*Where are you?*"

"*Victoria's Secret.*"

"*What's her secret, by the way?*"

"*She has a penis.*"

"*I copy.*"

"*No, Chardonnay, you paste. Call me at lunch.*"

While Aspen helped a customer upstairs, Ichika approached the desk with a water bottle. Today, Ichika wore all black, as if after a funeral. She lowered the bottle and watered a small container topped with soil sitting next to me. The container, wooden and rectangular, stood no higher than a toaster. The soil darkened from moisture, releasing an earthy aroma.

"What are you growing, Ichika?" I asked. "I've been wondering what the planter was."

"Some flower," she said.

"What kind of flower?"

"No. Sunflower."

"Oh, you're growing sunflowers?"

She nodded. "I love eating sunflower. Think to myself, why not grow? But two year, no sunflower. But I still water. Maybe one day, it grow."

"What kind of seeds did you use?"

"I buy in store in pouch. Already salt, roast."

"Wait," I said. "You planted already roasted and salted sunflowers?"

Ichika nodded, producing a bag of sunflower seeds from her pocket. "I love roast sunflower. You try." Ichika offered me the bag, but I shook my head.

"No, thank you, Ichika. I don't like sunflower seeds, and they usually add so much salt."

"Oh right. You, Cinnamon, and Aspen no eat. You want boyfriend. But I no have sunflower, and you no have boyfriend."

"That's right. Although we don't want to have boyfriends, we've decided. They're too much trouble."

"Everybody need boyfriend."

"That's what I thought, but men are horrible. Dating these days sucks."

"Grow sunflower suck, but I do anyway. I dream. If you never try find boyfriend, then you never find boyfriend."

That night, during our three-way phone call, I told the girls about my conversation with Ichika.

"She pressures everyone to find a boyfriend," Cinnamon said. "I think it's a Japanese thing."

"I can't believe she plants roasted seeds and expects flowers," I said. "Doesn't she know the seeds must be fresh? But for one hot second today, I felt like I had a mother or something. It was such a mother thing to talk about. Lucy was the same when I was her babysitter."

"Cookie is exactly the same," Aspen said. "Every time I visit, the first thing she asks is whether I found a boyfriend."

"Girls," Cinnamon said. "Can we please not talk about Ichika and Cookie? One's in a prison of her own mind, and the other one is in an actual prison. If you listen to them, you'll end up there too. Now that *that's* over with, let's finalize our beach plans for the Fourth. We should have mimosas while we're on the train."

"Where are we going?" I asked.

"Asbury Park in New Jersey," Cinnamon said. "Let's leave work early tomorrow, like two or three, and I'll take the fifth off—the two of you are already off—and we'll get us a cheap motel for two nights. Those in favor raise your hands. I see three hands. Great job, ladies."

I could barely sleep that night, imagining Asbury Park. Drinks would flow freely as the celebration of independence went on, loosening me up in an unexpected way. The moon would be barely visible over the ocean, a vague waxing crescent, the boardwalk teeming with action, with life. The three of us would walk, drunk, laughing, having a good time. At a souvenir vendor, we'd purchase trinkets to remember the night. I imagined a magnet for Aspen, a necklace for me, and a shot glass for Cinnamon.

For dinner, we'd have lobster in a buttery sauce, curly fries, and deep-fried Oreos or saltwater taffy for dessert. Fireworks would burst in the sky in rainbow colors, whistling from happiness, cheerful and bright. We would use the exploding night sky as a background for a million selfies, celebrating our nation's birthday, our independence.

Alas, that's not what happened.

Thirty-Three

During our train ride to Asbury Park, Aspen fell asleep on Cinnamon's shoulder. Unlike on a bus, where you always sit in a row, on New Jersey Transit trains, the back of a seat can be flipped to either side, so we'd flipped one and created a cozy nook, facing one another. Cinnamon had made mimosas at home in three dark tumblers, and we'd started sipping as soon as we claimed our seats.

"Lisa yelled at me for not washing the dishes and apologized this morning," I said.

"The old bag apologized … *again*?" Cinnamon said. "She needs a life."

"She hasn't left the house in weeks. She gets her groceries delivered. She puts our trash near our neighbor's door. She talks to guys on dating apps, and the only friend in her life is Lise or her mom on the phone."

"I guess I saw that one coming, Chardonnay. People like Lisa are morons. Like, who wants to be friends with someone like her? She just yells at you and then says she's sorry. It's so easy to apologize, but it's not easy not to mess shit up to begin with."

"You think so?"

"Absolutely. She clearly has psychopathic tendencies. Someone like her will mentally drain you, constantly get on your nerves, criticize, and *then* apologize. Once. Her subconsciousness clears while here you are, crying and feeling bad about yourself."

"How do you know all that?"

"Honey, I've met thousands of Lisas in Miami and New York. They're bloodsuckers who survive on young blood like you and me. Because we don't know any better and actually have aspirations, we come to big cities seeking success by sacrificing everything, blinded by inexperience. My first apartment in Miami, a 'Lisa' was charging me double what the apartment was worth. I didn't know any better. Same story in New York when I lived with another 'Lisa' on Ditmars in Astoria."

"You're saying Lisa overcharges my rent?"

"I would bet on it . . . all my money, honey."

"I have an excellent deal, Cinnamon. I only pay six hundred dollars, plus utilities."

"Lisa probably pays three times less. I promise you that. Lisas of the world typically end up friendless, miserable, or in jail. They're crooks like Cookie. That's why I live alone these days—because I won't let anyone take advantage of me. So watch out for her crocodile tears and apologies. A perfect friend doesn't apologize, Chardonnay. A perfect friend doesn't need to. Like, I can totally trust you. I know that. You'll never scam me."

"I trust you, too, Cinnamon."

"Good, because tonight is the night. We're going to a party."

"Where?"

"Do you trust me?"

"I trust you. I was just asking where we're going."

"You must trust me, Chardonnay, because I'm not Lisa, and I won't apologize the next day for something you agreed upon doing yourself."

I was so confused. "Agreed to do what?"

"You don't have to do it unless you want to."

"I will if I understand what you're talking about."

Cinnamon carefully pushed Aspen off her shoulder, letting her rest against the seat, and leaned in, whispering, "Molly."

"Who's Molly?" I whispered back.

"Molly as in MDMA."

"We're doing Molly?"

"Unless you don't want to. I totally understand if you don't."

"No, I want to. But I've never tried it."

"Well," she said, "Molly is literally pure MDMA, not bullshit ecstasy into which they add bath salts and whatnot. I've had the same dealer for years, and she brings the best stuff."

"What does Molly even do?"

"You love everything and everyone, and you want to listen to music and dance. It's not addictive either. It gives you a little high; that's all. You sure you wanna do it?"

"Positive."

"But it's your decision, Chardonnay. If something goes wrong, I won't apologize tomorrow like a 'Lisa.' This is your choice."

"I know."

Cinnamon leaned back, smiling, and raised her tumbler. We cheered from a distance, my heart rate accelerating from anticipation. There was only one other person in my life who tried party drugs, my roommate Liam, and I wanted to see what he thought. So I texted him.

He texted back, "*Molly is fun. Make sure you do it with someone you trust and drink plenty of water.*" With his message, he sent me a selfie from the beach wearing see-through swimwear. I locked my phone and glanced at Cinnamon, knowing perfectly well I could trust her 100 percent.

Thirty-Four

When the Molly kicked in, I wanted to be caressed and listen to music. My skin was soft and smooth, and it had never experienced such sensitivity before. There was no heartbeat in my chest, but my ears pulsated from the music, clean and repetitive, in sync with the light show. The dance floor was jam-packed, yet I was in my own bubble.

It felt exactly like the runner's high, and I told Cinnamon my observation.

"I love you," I told her. "I feel so much love right now."

Cinnamon didn't speak. While moving with the music, she positioned herself behind me, her fingertips on my shoulder blades. I was not rolling on Molly, I realized, just affectionate. I just loved everything. I was in love with Aspen, with Cinnamon, with my water bottle. This was what falling in love feels like! For the first time.

I let the sensation pass through me, that runner's high—oh wow, it felt like the runner's high. What a revelation! My body got high on "Molly" every time I went for a run. I found it funny and shared it with Cinnamon. I think I'd already mentioned that.

"I love you," I told her again. I touched her silky hair, running the beautiful auburn strands through my fingers.

We were bonding, the three of us. What takes months and years of friendship fast-forwarded at the speed of light. I'd known them for a millennium or longer. We'd been best friends since the last Ice Age, and I'd never loved anyone else. This was real love, certain, distinguishable.

"Let's take a break," Cinnamon said, and we glided across the dance floor, up the staircase, toward the bar.

"Drink up, ladies," she said. This was my fourth bottle of water, and it turned into a third trip to the bathroom.

"I don't want this night to end," I said. "I love you, girls."

I found it amusing that reality skipped as if a movie was being accelerated. First seconds, then entire minutes were missing—skipped and erased. The dance floor trembled beneath our feet . . . music . . . lights . . . other people.

I kissed Cinnamon. We walked up the staircase hand in hand. Why was the night accelerating? I checked my watch, and no, I was wrong—it'd only been thirty minutes. Time had slowed down, in fact.

I felt love for myself and the girls, with fervor, devotion, attachment. Such lust was true, pure happiness—bliss, an allegiance. No formula was needed, no cornerstones, no hatred toward my past. I loved my mother, and I finally respected her choice to leave me. Her circumstances disallowed her raising a child, and I'm A-OK. She wished only the best for me, knowing I'd find success in a better family, and I'd found them—Cinnamon and Aspen. My mother abandoned me out of love and integrity. And I finally understood what true, pure love for myself felt like, multiplied by a million. I was in paradise. I wanted to experience such love and tenderness for as long as I was conscious …

Thirty-Five

The euphoria lasted for several hours. Rolling came in waves, and it felt like absolute heaven, followed by some sort of soberness and normality. I felt this incredible, indescribable warmth inside my heart, wanting to cry from happiness to restore my emotional equilibrium. I exited my body and looked down at myself, watching my frozen body buried deep in ice. But an invisible ice pick and warmth were setting me free, tons of ice breaking apart and falling into the ocean …

Sleep never came. For hours, I twisted in bed, trying not to get bothered by my accelerated heartbeat. The ton of water consumed at the club sent me to the bathroom frequently. My tummy was bulged out from bloating. My pupils were dilated, and I kept clenching my jaw. Nausea brought me to the bathroom yet again, but weirdly, nothing came out. I drank orange juice to replenish my electrolytes, got under the covers, and sometime later, found myself back in the bathroom. We were sharing a bed,

Cinnamon and I, and we cuddled in between our bathroom visits.

"Cinnamon, I can't sleep," I whispered.

"Just try. Close your eyes," she said and embraced me harder, ready to hold me if I attempted an escape.

I opened my eyes, letting them adjust in the darkness of the room, an empty canvas. The dawn finally snuck through the cracks in the curtains, still bluish and vague, slowly painting the shapes in the room, stroke after stroke. The air conditioner stopped grumbling, finally reaching its auto-shutoff temperature. The sudden quietness was mollifying. Waves crashing against the beach took me back to my childhood in Orlando, distant yet dear to my heart. The beach holds its record of "happy firsts" for me. The first kiss with a boy—and now a girl. I remembered how after taking Molly, all inhibitions left me. That kiss, however, didn't mean anything. Yet it meant everything at the same time. I lost my virginity to a man on the beach, and last night, I lost it to Molly. Uncanny parallels.

I opened my eyes. Sunshine had filled the room with morning light, and the air conditioner had resumed its annoying grumbling, blocking outside noises. I couldn't sleep. I sat up with my back against the headboard, taking in the room. Aspen was curled into a ball in the bed closest to the window, the air conditioner blasting cold air over her. I covered her with an extra blanket and returned to the bed without waking Cinnamon.

The motel room eerily resembled Lyon's. Floral bedspread patterns, mismatched particleboard furniture in dark brown or coffee, mustard carpeting that resembled and felt like sand. A damp, musty smell persisted on the pillows and now on my skin. When the air conditioner shut off, life outside resumed. Merciless waves of the Atlantic Ocean, shrill yells of young kids, crooning of seagulls.

I grabbed my phone from the nightstand, and it lighted up, showing the time: 8:15 a.m., July 4. Independence Day.

I wanted to cry for no apparent reason. It felt as if happiness had completely abandoned me, leaving me alone in a dark void, deep in space on another planet, freezing and terrifying. I conjured up positive memories—nights out with my girlfriends, running in Central Park early in the morning, the aroma of cherry trees blooming in spring—but like a psychopath, I felt nothing. Except suicidal thoughts. Life didn't seem to matter anymore. Like a long game of Monopoly, for twenty-six years, I'd struggled and fought for my place on this planet, working every day, saving money, and making friends. With one sweep, the board had been emptied, game pieces gone, jaws of a black abyss open wide and ready to swallow. I felt mentally and physically depleted, a new low of despair, something I'd never felt before, another first the beach can have on its record of firsts. The feeling of despair was followed by absurd, unexplainable, terrifying self-loathing. I'd hated people in the past, but this was the next level of hate. As if life had collected all the hate in the world and bottled it. And I drank it all.

My hands shook from fear as I texted Liam, seeking an explanation for these abhorrent, suicidal thoughts. Anything would help. I was scared to die, but that was what my mind wanted.

To my surprise, Liam replied right away. "*Your serotonin and dopamine levels are low. You'll be fine. Text me if you need anything.*"

Liam's explanation made sense, and I somehow found comfort in his reply. Science makes me wary, but it pacified me like a parent soothing a scared child. I'd heard of serotonin before. Serotonin and dopamine are happiness hormones, and they were responsible for the euphoria I felt after running. Why was I low in serotonin? I needed to learn right away.

I searched online, and a variety of sites linked Molly to depression and suicidal thoughts. At least I was not the only one.

"You can call MDMA a neurotransmitter catcher, so to speak," one user, Dan White, said in a comment. "Once inside your body, you basically overdose on happiness provided by the neurotransmitters serotonin and dopamine. You experience increased affection. When your body produces these neurotransmitters naturally, it recycles them safely, trying to keep them at steady levels. On Molly, your brain can't recycle them, as the recycling pathways are blocked by the drug. That's why you get a feeling of incredible euphoria, all these happiness particles accelerating in the networks of your brain. When the drug wears off, the brain is finally able to recycle the excess neurotransmitters. About twelve hours after the dose, you're left with such a low amount of serotonin and dopamine, you feel like you suddenly want to kill yourself."

Thank you, Dan White, for mansplaining in such easy language. His comment literally described how I felt—that sudden urge of sadness and thoughts of suicide. OK, then. This feeling would pass with time. So long as I occupied my hands with something other than weapons that cut human flesh. At that moment, my fingers resembled claws, and I envisioned inserting them in my neck, ripping my head off. Quick, forceful, but manageable, like ripping off a Band-Aid.

The air conditioner whirred back to life yet again, loud and obnoxious. Like with my head, I wanted to rip it off the wall and throw it into the ocean, strong like Thor. I jumped from the bed and shut it off, trembling with wrath.

"There, you stupid hooker," I muttered and hit it lightly with my palm.

I jumped back. Oh my God. I was angry at an appliance. What was happening to me? I looked at my hands, but they were not mine. They were the devil's, and he wanted to punish me with them.

My eyes juggled between two beds. Aspen was motionless, still curled up in a ball like a cat. Cinnamon resembled an angel, with her silky hair covering one side of her face. I felt love for them, without blaming them for anything. I wished Cinnamon had mentioned the side effects, especially the void, but I signed up for it myself.

An idea for how to fix myself arrived suddenly, but it was controversial in my mind. It was something I'd never done before. I wanted to punish myself physically. My mind believed it would help. I imagined the kleptomaniac choking me, humping me from behind the way he wished, while pain paralyzed my body. I imagined the misogynist tying me up, the rope cutting through my skin, him whipping a helpless girl without mercy.

As children, we learn that crime is followed by punishment. One of my foster moms, a big, strong woman, beat me with a belt for bad grades. In school, we end up in detention for fighting a classmate. Committing a crime lands us in jail. But what about us adults? Do we know how to discipline ourselves?

I craved punishment to remind myself a crime had been committed, a crime against myself that had put me in this void with suicidal thoughts. How dare I did this to myself? While it seemed counterproductive to punish myself further after punishing my mental health, it somehow made sense. That was what the mind wanted.

If we punish each other frequently, is it possible we punish ourselves even more frequently? As soon as we find happiness, we feel immoral that the rest of the world lives in despair, and we find ways to sabotage that happiness, such as by soaking in alcohol, which only exacerbates the situation. Is it possible, perchance, that Cookie craved punishment for exploiting young girls and ended up at Rikers because she sought redemption? And finally, is it possible my mom felt undeserving as a person and punished herself by abandoning her child as her punishment?

Was Cinnamon right that Lisa and Lise took advantage of me by overcharging rent and felt guilty about it? Lisa cleaned the apartment and Lise brought me gifts—to clear their conscience. Is anyone genuinely kind simply because of their nature? Or are we all selfish, seeking ways to forgive ourselves? Does winter exist without spring? And does crime exist without punishment? Most important, does self-hatred exist without self-love?

Can you become an adult if you're never a parent? Can you become kind if you've never been cruel? Can you ever be anything unless you've literally been its opposite?

I turned on the water in the bathtub and the bathroom sink to block out any suspicious noises that I expected would follow. I stood in front of the mirror, embarrassed to look at myself, as what I was about to do was beyond humiliating. Was I really doing this? Yes, I needed to take a hard look at myself. I looked in the mirror.

My face looked ugly, swollen, misshapen, with bags under my eyes. My formerly sunken cheeks were plump and yellowish, a zit growing near my nose. My hair resembled thatch, sticking out in an unflattering way. My beauty had faded in a blink of an eye, and I was an ugly girl now. All these years spent running and starving and puking to look good—gone in a finger snap. My pupils were dilated, my tummy protruding. I definitely deserved it, so I slapped my cheek.

Quick and fast.

"Shit," I whispered.

The hit stung. It stung a lot, but it also felt good to feel pain. I deserved it. I slapped myself again, only harder—but it was the misogynist slapping me. My head hurt. *No, please, do it again, and again. The other cheek, sir.* My heart rate accelerated. I was possessed by someone. *Please, don't kill me, but punish me all you want.*

Slap after slap left me feeling undeniably better, but slapping wasn't enough punishment. The misogynist spanked my ass with his strong hand.

I stepped into the shower and closed my eyes, letting the running water wash away my sins. I needed to hurt myself more and more, and even if the kleptomaniac wasn't here, I imagined he was, lathering my body with soap, lubricating me before he inserted himself in clandestine parts of me that had been unavailable to him. The kleptomaniac punished me by turning the hot water off. I was left standing under a cold stream, shivering, my hands turning blue. I was embarrassed by myself as I let his hands squeeze my neck. With the other, he entered any part he desired. I was his slave, he told me, so I had to stop crying. I belonged to him now.

Thirty-Six

While drying myself off with a motel-provided towel, rough and prickly, I mentally felt better. Physically, however, I craved more damage. But invisible, hurtless damage. I craved dissolution in alcohol, hoping a high would diminish the void in my head. Void from some deeply rooted pain. Some people would call that sadness, hopelessness, or depression. What I felt, however, was depression having depression.

Yesterday, we filled up Cinnamon's cooler with three bottles of cheap rosé for the beach, using ice from the ice machine outside. The ice had partially melted, and the three bottles floated freely like three ships in the freezing Atlantic. I removed one bottle, and while it was dripping all over the carpet, I carried it to the bathroom. For some reason, I wanted to keep looking at my reflection, straight into my eyes. As soon as I moved away from the mirror, reality blended with imagination, and I couldn't tell truth from fiction. While I wiped the bottle with a towel, I noticed the label, where a drawn petite woman on the beach held a glass out while a waiter in a tux poured from the bottle. Like a suggestion on how the rosé should be served. Not even in our wildest dreams would a man serve us. I twisted the top off and started drinking straight from the rim. Acid hit my throat. The wine was dry and vile, the complete opposite of what wine supposedly stands for, a classy beverage served with a fine meal. Five years ago, I took to chardonnay like a stripper to a stripper pole. I'd never tried fine wine. Wine was for getting drunk, and that I accomplished easily when the last drop reached my mouth. The void inside me had been filled, but not with happiness the way I'd imagined, but with rage I couldn't fully understand.

I packed in haste, thinking how much I despised Aspen and Cinnamon, two sleeping beauties who were to blame. Before I killed myself, I wanted to murder them first. *Please, stop thinking about murdering anyone,* I told myself. I dressed, grabbed my bag, and left, slamming the door on the way out.

Just like I expected, my phone rang by the time I reached the train station. According to the schedule, the train to New York ran once per hour and was supposed to arrive in five minutes. Cinnamon called again, and I picked up.

"Chardonnay, did you go to the beach without us?"

"Screw you, Cinnamon, with all my heart. I hate you so freaking much. I hope you rot in hell."

"Jesus Christ. What is the matter?"

"You wanna know what the matter is? How about you not telling me that the aftereffect of using Molly is suicide?"

"Chardonnay, please, don't do anything stupid."

"Oh yeah, like being friends with you, for example?"

"Come back. Let's talk about it."

"I'm through with you and that dumb Aspen."

"Honey, you're overreacting. What you're experiencing is normal after Molly."

"If it's normal, you should have warned me about it."

"I didn't realize it would affect you in such a way. Stay where you are, and I'll come get you."

"You don't know where I am."

"We're sharing our location with each other. I'm on my way now."

I hung up and shut off my phone. I couldn't see her, or I was going to claw her eyes out, after which I'd throw her under the train. I ran to the end of the platform, remembering belatedly how we'd shared our locations with each other last night, just in case we got lost at the club.

Thankfully, I heard baritone tooting in the distance, and the train appeared. I jumped inside. As we started moving, relief washed over me, and as we bypassed the middle of the platform, I saw Cinnamon on the phone, freaking out. She didn't notice me, and I sneered. *You deserve that, you stupid traitor,* I told her in my head while opening a second bottle of wine, which I'd snatched from the cooler.

Part Six

Crime and Punishment

What you resist persists.

—CARL JUNG

Thirty-Seven

I returned home at noon. Thankfully, I'd only had a few sips of rosé and fell asleep on the train, whose rocking and shaking lulled me to sleep. I was thirsty and needed to use the bathroom so badly that I could barely walk from the subway.

Lisa greeted me in the kitchen while sticking a piece of celery in the juicer. The kitchen counter was full of fresh produce, from cucumbers to ginger to leafy greens.

While in the john, I heard her say, "I thought you were in New Jersey until tomorrow."

Couldn't she wait until I finished? God. As I exited, I gulped two cups of water, then sat on a barstool.

"Cinnamon is a total hellcat," I said as Lisa turned the juicer off. "You were right."

"Why? What happened?"

"She drugged me."

"Are you serious?"

"We did Molly last night, my first time. But Cinnamon never told me about the side effects—like suicidal thoughts. I'm feeling so low right now, Lisa. I've never felt this way before."

"I'm sorry," she said with a grin.

"What? Don't tell me you told me so. I'm really not in the mood for lectures right now. I know I messed up.

Why did I think Cinnamon had changed from her cocaine days? She said so herself. Once a cheater, always a cheater."

"I don't know what that means."

"Don't worry about it. What are your plans today?"

"Lise and Liam wanna go to Astoria Park to watch the fireworks. Wanna join?"

"Yes, thank you. What should I do about work? Should I quit?"

"No, don't quit. Talk with her. Tell her why you're upset. Make her apologize."

"Oh, Cinnamon doesn't apologize. She said so herself. In fact, when I told her that you apologized after our fight—"

"She what?" Lisa said. "You told her I apologized?"

"Well, I told her what had happened between us and that in the end, you apologized. That's what happened."

"I apologized for Lise. I didn't want us to fight, and Lise takes everything personally, like a complete baby. I *still* think I was right. I always stand behind what I say."

"You didn't mean to apologize?"

"I wanted to make things better, is all. I still stand behind everything I said."

"I see. You still think I'm fake and should date fat assholes in sandals. Nobody tells the truth anymore these days."

"Lindsay, don't get upset. The world doesn't revolve around you. We all have lives, and as long as the four of us live together under one roof, I want us to be civil. That's my bottom line."

"Got it," I said and stood up.

"Where are you going?"

"My bedroom."

"Lindsay, don't get mad."

"That's what you always say. Maybe it's time, Lisa, you stop making people mad."

Thirty-Eight

I cranked up the air conditioner in my bedroom and lay down. The sheets felt warm and damp, but the cold air helped cool me down. I checked my phone, expecting to find a million messages from Aspen and Cinnamon. But no such messages arrived.

Were they for real?

I stalked their social media. Aspen posted a selfie from the beach with the caption, "Sunshine with my bestie. You're either with us or against us."

Rot in hell, I thought and closed my eyes. That was a message for me, a message showing me their superiority.

That proved how immature they were, and I wasn't going to fall into their trap.

I also hate it when people like Lisa tell me not to get mad after telling me what a piece of shit I really am. *Oh, I'm not supposed to get mad?* OK, thanks for the tip.

What I hate worse is reading fairy tales, and it's two-fold. First, they all start with "A long, long time ago . . ." Please be specific. *You're* the freaking storyteller. You should know when the story takes place. And I know for a fact it wasn't a long, long time ago. Right? And if you really don't know, either make something up or tell a story you know is true. I also hate fairy tales because, like social media, they project unrealistic expectations about life. For instance, every girl can become a princess after cleaning houses or kissing frogs. *So* far-fetched. I don't care that they're fairy tales. They're still projections of reality, just like social media. Aspen and Cinnamon were angry with me for sure, but they acted like they were having a good time.

So now I lived in hell at home, at work, *and* in my head. The three of us had taken the next day off, but what would I do afterward? I picked up my phone and called Lyon. After several rings, his phone went to voice mail, and I cleared my throat, saying, "Lyon, hi, this is Lindsay. I'm not feeling well today—fever and stuff, so I won't come to work for the next few days. I may have the flu. I'm sorry for calling on a holiday, but the store is closed, and I don't know how else to let you know. I'll see you when I feel better."

Calling in appeared effortless, but how would I "call in" from my roommates? I took my second shower that day, avoiding speaking to Lisa, who was still juicing. I put on a top and shorts, then took the small purse that Lise had gifted me and added cash, a credit card, and my driver's license, after which I left the apartment, my phone still resting on my bed and the air conditioner running for when I returned from Randy's, hopefully not alone. Before leaving, I texted the misogynist and told him where I'd be if he wanted to come say hi.

Thirty-Nine

I woke up the next day with the misogynist in my bed. The previous night, I'd given him what he craved. I can't believe we actually talked at Randy's, and he wanted me to get to know him. He was from Plain, Wisconsin, and exactly looked the part—plain and boring. But someone who could punish me, which is what I craved.

I checked my phone and found numerous missed calls from Lise and Liam but nothing from Aspen and Cinnamon. Before going to sleep last night, I'd taken painkillers, and I woke up feeling fine. A little woozy, but nothing a cup of coffee couldn't fix.

"Get up," I told Miso and poked him with my fingers. "I need to go to work."

He groaned. "I thought you were off today."

"Yes, but I was wrong. Just received a message from my boss. Needs me there stat."

He twisted under the sheets, sleep lines crisscrossing his face. "One more time, Leslie, and then I'll go," he said and hopped on top of me. Before I could protest, his tongue was deep in my mouth with his morning breath from hell. For the next five minutes, I didn't really care what he did to me. Suddenly, his face twitched, and it was all over with. He quickly dressed, put on sandals—oh my Lord, I thought—and left, saying, "Text me later, Leslie."

I didn't bother correcting him, dearly hoping to never see his disgusting face again, repulsive, in a way, like his personality. Physically, he looked like a guy I wanted to date. He was talk, dark, and handsome. He worked out regularly ... protruding veins, low body fat.

When he left, the reality of loneliness hit me. For some reason, I envisioned Cookie at Rikers, alone behind bars, and in one quick second, I stood under the shower. I'd never been to Rikers and wondered how visitations even worked. While having my coffee, I learned online that the

Q100 goes from Astoria straight to Rikers Island. I called ahead to make sure visitations were allowed, but what happened next was a punishment in and of itself. At first, I wondered why women on the bus stared at me for the entirety of the ride. I knew nothing about a strict dress code: no leggings, no dresses (what I wore), no V-necks or bright colors. No ponytails or buns. For those who wear tight clothes, an extra-large, green neon tee is given, but because my knees showed, it wouldn't work anyway. I didn't bring an ID, which was required, and jewelry was not allowed. How come Aspen never mentioned how hard it was to actually get in? (Unless you committed a crime; then voilà.)

On the way back, I felt stupid. There's a reason I took Molly, I realized. I wasn't smart at all because an intelligent girl would never make a foolish mistake. If I had access to the internet, then why wasn't I using it? At least I tried seeing Cookie. I barely understood why. Did I seek advice from a motherly figure after having a fight with my friends? What could a woman with a name like Cookie possibly teach me about life?

Forty

In the afternoon, I texted my frenemy Chloe and asked her to lunch. I just needed some friendly face, even if half the time she hated me. At least she hated me to my face, unlike Lisa and the passive-aggressive Aspen with her selfie captures.

I now regretted quitting the live-in babysitting job. I left because I wished to live on my own, but I was clearly incapable of independence.

We met in Central Park. Chloe used to be a large girl, but she'd lost seventy pounds, and she'd started growing out her hair. I secretly judged her for her inheritance and commitment to her workout routine. I was jealous that she lived with her mother. I wanted to tell her everything, from my fights with Lisa to taking Molly with Aspen and Cinnamon. Yet I felt embarrassed about disclosing the absurd reality of my situation.

"You seem much happier," Chloe randomly said as we walked through the park. "I guess the four cornerstones of happiness worked out for you."

"I think the cornerstones were a stupid idea. I no longer believe happiness can be put in a box like that. I now draw happiness from other sources, like self-help books and running and meeting old friends. I'm trying to connect to the past and even tried visiting Cookie in jail."

"I *live* by your formula of happiness, Lindsay. Except the fourth cornerstone for me is not a relationship but peace—simple as that—peace. So long as I don't fight with my mom, I'm the happiest person, but when we get into an argument, I lose it and become mad at others."

"What about a job?"

"You were right. I don't need a job per se. I have the money, and I even won the lottery on top of that. The universe is telling me to do something. So I'll travel."

"How much money did you win?"

"Two hundred and fifty thousand dollars! Can you believe it?"

My eyes fell out of my head. "Congratulations! It proves that money always follows money. Where are you going?"

"I'm going to Italy, then to India, and then to Bali to realize my *Eat, Pray, Love* fantasy. I've finally finished it per your recommendation, and you were right. You knew me when I still didn't. I have to travel and see the world."

"I told you that?"

"Yes, you did. Why have all this money if I can't see the world? Find my passion. And I'm sorry if I was mean to you. I was just upset with myself and projected my anger."

"I'm sorry too."

That evening at home, I wondered if Chloe was right. I felt miserable fighting with Lise and Cinnamon and briefly contemplated whether apologizing truly worked.

I texted Lisa and Cinnamon the same thing: "*Sorry about yesterday.*"

Lisa replied with a heart emoji and said: "*I understand.*"

Cinnamon replied as well: "*Come to Randy's.*"

I felt light as a feather—light.

But of course, Cinnamon didn't let me off the hook so easily.

Forty-One

Unlike Lisa, Cinnamon planned to punish me for a long, long time. I could tell from her demeanor as soon as she laid her blue eyes on me at Randy's, a mixture of regret and despise. She and Aspen sat in our usual spot at the bar's corner by the entrance, two martinis in front of them.

I opened with, "I'm sorry about yesterday morning."

"What the fuck happened?" Cinnamon asked.

"I don't know. I woke up not feeling like myself. I still don't know if I feel like myself."

"Girl, I warned you on the train that if something happened, you couldn't blame me for it."

"I know. That's why I feel bad about what happened. And I have a plan. Will you forgive me if, for the next few months, all my commission is yours?"

She thought about it, lips pursed. "That could work, Chardonnay. But you have to promise that something like this won't ever happen again."

"I promise."

"We were so worried about you. We thought you were going to jump in front of a train. I thought I'd never see you again."

"I didn't mean to make you feel that way," I said. "Again, I wasn't myself."

"Well, it's not Molly, Chardonnay; it's you. Molly helps you understand who you really are. And you're such a textbook Aries, it's crazy. So impulsive and independent. That's what we love about you. Right, Aspen?"

"Right," Aspen said.

"Just work on your anger," Cinnamon continued. "That's the beauty of Molly. It teaches you about your imperfections. Now that you know you're a raging bitch, work on yourself. Remember everything that happened, step by step, and try to fix every single mistake. You stormed off, stole wine from the cooler, yelled at your friend. You can learn from your behavior and prevent future mistakes."

"I understand," I said.

"Great. I don't want to talk about this anymore."

Part Seven

Transformation

Water surrounds the lotus flower,
but does not wet its petals.
—GAUTAMA BUDDHA

Forty-Two

In the next three weeks that followed, I went through a transformation, leaving the old Chardonnay behind. The void I felt after the first night of Molly had remained deep inside me, hollowing me out further until no more humanity remained. Awake in the morning, I would stare at the ceiling, and even if there were reasons to get up—work, friends, life—those reasons seemed meaningless. Yes, the meaning of life had been stripped off like old plaster. I stared at the ceiling, blaming drugs and condemning myself.

I'd learned everything there was to know about neurotransmitters. For example, a lack of L-tryptophan (found in meat) causes low levels of serotonin and dopamine. Because the neurotransmitters develop in the gut, gut health is key to mental health. I stocked up on L-tryptophan, probiotics, B-12, and various over-the-counter serotonin-boosting supplements. However, eating meat daily for a girl who survived mainly on kale was out of character for me. Even Liam made a face one day as I made a steak for the third time in a row.

"Are you fattening up for the winter?" he joked.

"I did a blood test," I lied, "and they said I was low in B-12. Plus, the meat is pasture raised and organic, which helps reduce global warming. We must help the world, my friend. That's the first cornerstone of happiness."

"What are you talking about? Are you high?"

"Eating animals that are pasture raised helps global warming. I learned that from a documentary."

"You're so weird these days," he said and went to his room.

Running stopped bringing me joy, but I powered through without a reward, for I no longer could reach that runner's high. Perhaps permanent damage had been done to my neurotransmitter receptors. Serotonin and dopamine levels stay constant, and typically, running elevates them slightly and momentarily, bringing a quick (but worthy) moment of bliss. On Molly, that level rises to such incredible heights that no amount of running could bring that joy ever again. Yoga and meditation had become chores, and reading self-help books was now an even bigger obsession.

I kept my raging moods from Aspen and Cinnamon and from Lisa and Lise.

Chloe was in Italy, eating pasta every day, posting hundreds of pictures.

Nikita wanted to see how my credit score was going and tell me about her exciting relationship with Joaquin, but I couldn't be genuinely happy while in such a deep, unhappy pit myself.

Candace attended gala after gala, trying to raise money for dozens of charities, sacrificing her own transition in the process.

I stalked the three of them on social media, jealous of their simple, yet healthy and unpretentious lives. I was sure they'd never experienced the void I felt. They seemed happy. Or whatever the typical happiness means before the void takes over your body.

Randy's helped fill the void in the evening, but I felt like the shell of myself during the day.

Unbeknownst to anyone, not even Aspen and Cinnamon, I started making my morning coffee Irish. That alone wouldn't necessarily make me happy, but shopping for clothes at lunch would.

Working with Ichika had become a total nightmare. That woman had never stopped smiling, and her bright disposition darkened mine, even if simply by contrast. I now understood why Aspen and Cinnamon hated her from the beginning. I hated everything about her. The way she walked, the way she dressed, her funny accent.

One time, I was at Lyon's with just Ichika, without customers, Lyon, or the girls. It was pouring rain, rivers gushing down the boulevard. Astoria was gloomy and desolated, but I was stuck at work with the happiest woman on Earth.

I stretched a fake smile, gulped some Irish coffee, and said, "Ichika, you're always so happy. Are you taking any medication?"

She smiled, as always, and replied, "I no always happy, Lizzy."

"You always smile and seem genuinely happy."

"I smile, but I no always happy. But I smile, and you think I happy."

"So you just pretend you're happy all the time?"

"No pretend. I happy, but no always happy."

"I see," I said.

"Everything OK?" she asked while a thunderstorm rumbled outside.

"It'll sound stupid, Ichika, but I feel like my heart is shrinking somehow."

"No stupid, Lizzy. Heart squeeze when you cry or upset. It feel like it squeeze."

"Yes, exactly."

"You stretch heart. I teach. Laugh as hard as you can. Like this."

Ichika starts giggling like a geisha girl, which turns into a laugh and then an uncontrollable hoot.

"Now you try," she said.

"I can't. That's ridiculous."

"Try, Lizzy. It help."

For the next five minutes, we laughed like two fools until lightning struck and we both gasped. Outside, crackling was followed by an explosion of thunder. When I opened my eyes, I clutched Ichika from fear. I was laughing and crying. It felt ridiculous and embarrassing, and I was grateful nobody was there to watch us.

"See?" Ichika said. "Cry—good. It mean heart no more squeeze. Heart open."

Another day, she'd been harassing me about why I didn't have a boyfriend. For women of her generation, a relationship is the most vital part of life. I watched documentaries about it. In the past, women sought companionship and compatibility to survive through wars and to protect heirs. Now, women were looking for love and romance, which, according to historians, had never existed before. Love and romance had been created by the feminists as a reason not to marry men. Plus, in modern society, women occupied high posts and could live independently. But it was hard to relay that information to Ichika. I mean, what was my love life to her? How did that bring her any happiness?

"Lizzy," she asked me, "what your name mean?"

"I don't know," I said, then pulled out my phone, looking it up. "What does Ichika mean?"

"One thousand flower."

"One thousand sunflowers?" I asked, and we both laughed for no particular reason.

"*Lindsay* means 'lake,'" I told her, reading about my name online.

"*Mizumi*," she said.

"What's that?"

"*Lake* in Japanese. That your nickname now. OK?"

Another day, I had to deal with a difficult customer who purchased a sofa from me and wanted to get it delivered to Fort Salonga on Long Island. The customer was a woman in a burka, and she continued talking on the phone with someone the entire time while at Lyon's. I made the sale and called Juan to ask him about delivery availability. He told me Fort Salonga was out of our delivery zone. *Great,* I thought, wishing someone had mentioned that to me before. I flagged down Ichika, who explained to the woman that our sister store was located on Long Island in Huntington and that they might deliver. I called the store, but the rude girl with a New York Italian accent who picked up the phone said, "We can't just transfer a sale like that. Send her here, and we'll sell her the couch." Without waiting for a reply, she hung up. The woman in a burka went through everything in her arsenal: "Can you make an exception?" I said no. "I need to speak to the manager." I called Ichika. "You shouldn't be in sales if you can't possibly satisfy the customer."

The situation was more than I could bear. With what I was going through, I could get upset just if a sad song came on the radio, let alone an angry customer who got personal. Little mishaps annoyed me to no end, and big accidents brought me to tears.

It culminated with us refunding her. She then added that she'd never return, including notifying her friends.

My head started pounding, but Ichika approached me and touched my shoulders gently.

"Mizumi," she said, "Wonder Woman pose."

"What do you mean?"

She pushed on my shoulder blades with her thumbs, and my chest automatically moved forward, straightening my back.

"See?" she asked. "When you angry, Wonder Woman pose help."

Ichika placed her arms on her waist, chest out, legs shoulder-width apart. "You stand like Wonder Woman," she said. "Special power pose. Make you strong. You try."

Just like with everything Ichika did, I found it incredibly silly and embarrassing. But as I stood there, holding the Wonder Woman pose, an invisible force rushed through me, followed by a feeling of lightness.

Forty-Three

I knew what I craved, but I feared to admit it. I wanted to experience that Molly high, that love, once again. I read online that after the first time, each consequent one fades in comparison. I wasn't sure how Aspen and Cinnamon could endure life normally while I felt like a drug addict. Was I simply weaker than them, or was it because I'd only tried it once, and they were seasoned, so to speak?

I sought a perfect opportunity to ask Aspen and Cinnamon whether they wanted to go clubbing again. I feared, however, they'd suspect my conniving ways, and I dearly hoped one of them would suggest it herself. During outings at Randy's, I threw in clues suggesting Molly, like, "I wish we were dancing right now." Or, "Have you ever watched *The Unsinkable Molly Brown*?" Or, "Let's have Mexican for dinner. I'm craving mole." But the girls never seemed to catch the bait.

Finally, during one of our nightly three-way calls that had become more of a nuance than a pleasure for their simple routineness, I said, "Cinnamon, my roommate Liam wants to know the name of your dealer. He asked me to ask you. He needs Molly for some Fire Island party he's attending."

"I can get it for him, but I can't give him the number."

"Why not?"

"Just in case. Not that I distrust you or Liam but because my dealer asked me not to."

"I understand."

"How much does Liam want?"

"I don't know. Enough for three people."

"Well, everyone is different, Chardonnay. Just ask him whether he wants one bag or two."

"How much is a bag?"

"Fifty bucks."

"Did we take a bag last time in Asbury Park, or did we take more?" I asked, then bit my lip, my forehead sweaty.

"I think we took a bag, yeah," Cinnamon said. "I'll get a couple of bags, then, just in case we also wanna go clubbing sometime. But no funny business this time, Chardonnay."

"I'd like to," Aspen said.

"Me too," I said as if it were the last thing on my mind.

"How about Friday, August first?" Cinnamon asked. "Lyon is going out of town, so we can either close the next day or just not show up. Ichika can work all she wants."

"Why August first?" Aspen asked.

"It's National Girlfriends Day!"

Forty-Four

When I started rolling, I cried, for finally, I felt normal again. I'd tried Molly for the first time a month prior. My body craved this surge, neurotransmitters trapped in my brain, bouncing around with love and happiness, unrecyclable glee, nonstop affection.

According to the comments online, it was normal for the high to be less strong compared with the first time.

My heart felt open, the emptiness inside me overflowing with love and empathy. I suspected regrets would follow and eat me alive, but I really didn't care. I knew I acted like an addict, but I rejected common sense because a higher force was pulling my strings. My body craved love—true love—and now I was dancing. I felt like I belonged on Earth. I treasured and forgave my mom, dearly hoping she felt content. I forgave everyone in my life, including myself, forgiving every little mistake. What an incredible night—a night of forgiveness. It felt different this time. Perhaps it was a different cocktail of drugs—I'd read Molly is seldom pure, and other drugs, like cocaine and speed, are typically added. Whatever was in the second cocktail made me feel invincible. Rolling was coming in waves like the first time, but that night, I was absolutely sure I could keep it together afterward. I mean, I drank alcohol but wasn't an alcoholic. I shopped for clothes but wasn't a shopaholic. And therefore if I took Molly once a month, it didn't—from a technical standpoint—make me a drug addict.

I arrived home at five in the morning, no longer rolling but tired and unable to sleep. I felt bloated again but incredibly content and satisfied. I gave my brain what it wanted—a high—and dearly hoped my brain would give me what I needed—my happiness back.

At nine in the morning, still awake and wired, that insatiable craving for punishment arrived. It was constant, nagging, and had to happen immediately. I thought it was just a fluke the first time, but now I knew it came with the whole package. You want to feel extreme happiness? Now pay for it. Perhaps Cinnamon had been correct and Molly shows who you really are, and in reality, I wasn't strong and confident. I was insecure.

When that craving came, I realized it had nothing to do with punishing myself. It was about punishing the girl who had made me who I was today. I wanted to travel back in time and find myself dancing on a stripper pole in Astoria. I wanted to smack that little twat's face and tell her, *You're a piece of shit, Chardonnay. You're ruining my life by destroying yours. Get off the freaking pole, or you'll end up in agony, you selfish tramp.*

That's why I was such a failure, I realized. Nobody helped me understand who I was while growing up. I had to starve myself to death—trying to fit into the image of perfection. I needed perfection after being left unwanted in the hospital, beaten by a foster mom, and touched by rich old men.

I wanted to punish her, but I wasn't sure how. Young Chardonnay wanted to find real love and finish college to become somebody. To help young girls like herself to get out of poverty. To create some sort of nonprofit organization that could help abandoned children feel loved and indispensable.

"*Well, you know what,*" I told young Chardonnay. "*Forget your dreams because you don't deserve them! I'm going to become such a shithead, you will regret getting on that pole.*"

I wanted to ruin her irresponsible body. I texted the misogynist, precisely the person who stood against her beliefs, an arrogant douchebag who cared about nothing but his Greek-god body.

I said: "*Hey, up for some afternoon fun at your place? You can do whatever you want to me. I'm up for any fantasy.*"

If he didn't reply in the next five minutes, I would text the kleptomaniac next. And if that failed, I would reinstall the apps and find someone random.

Thankfully, the misogynist replied: "*Send me a naked picture.*" He followed up with a row of naked mirror selfies. He had an incredible body, but twelve pictures seemed excessive. I wondered how many he took daily, the narcissistic asshole. I really didn't care. I wanted young Chardonnay to suffer the way she deserved to. I undressed and snapped a bunch of pictures while covering my face.

I added: "*Chardonnay has been a bad girl. Will you punish her the way you wanted?*"

"*I want to tie her up.*"

"*Chardonnay deserves it.*"

"*Come over in an hour while I get ready.*" With that, he sent his address.

Forty-Five

My legs unwillingly carried me through the streets of Astoria toward his apartment, past the train tracks. I didn't want to do this, and I was scared. My body craved punishment, and that was the arrangement, the deal we'd made. Happiness costs money. Right now, I had to pay the price with my body. While the misogynist was getting ready, I'd made two cocktails at nine in the morning. Thankfully, everyone else was asleep and didn't see me.

Alcohol helped me with courage.

For this time of the morning, the humidity seemed excessive. Runners and early risers swooshed beside me, but the streets were mostly empty. After all, it was Saturday morning. And I felt drunk. I wanted to get slapped again and whatever else the misogynist craved. I wanted to be at a man's mercy. I did some reading online, wondering why I craved humiliation. Turns out, there are hundreds of communities devoted to sadomasochism, and plenty of ideas exist. In simple terms, we may crave humiliation because we crave punishment for something we did wrong. Other times, it's about giving up control. There was a reason I'd renamed myself as Chardonnay, who was a version of me, and that's who was getting punished today.

My legs shook as I rang his bell.

"Who is it?" his voice came, distorted through the intercom.

"Chardonnay."

He buzzed me in, and I walked up to the second floor, my heart fluttering in my chest. My head was spinning.

His door stood ajar. I waited a few seconds, taking five deep breaths. As I walked in, I heard him say, "Come to the bedroom to your left."

His living room was cramped with furniture and was dark. I took off my heels and proceeded toward the bedroom. He waited in the doorway, shirtless, in gym shorts.

"Hi," I said. "Call me Chardonnay."

"Hey," he said. "I'm going to put a blindfold on you. If you don't feel comfortable, just let me know."

"I'm comfortable."

When he covered my eyes, he pushed me from behind and said, "Take your top off and get on the bed."

I wore a black crop top and jean shorts, no underwear. I slipped the top off and stepped back, touching the bed behind me. I lowered my palms on the top of the bed and sat down. I heard him fumble out of his shorts, then approach me.

"Get down," he demanded. "On your knees."

For the next two hours, I was his blowup toy. I'd exited my body, watching myself being manhandled roughly, the way he wanted. He knew I was drunk and that yesterday, I was on Molly.

"I love drunk, submissive slaves like you," he said. "You'll do anything I'll say."

What followed was more than I expected or could handle, but I tried my best not to cry. He loved me on my knees, but he also loved hitting. After thirty minutes, I wanted him to finish, and I moaned, saying so.

"Not yet," he said, throwing me back on the bed, choking my neck.

That's what I'd signed up for, and I had to finish. I wanted to give up, but he kept going and going and going.

I was hurt, exhausted, and on the verge of tears when, suddenly, he pushed me down on my knees, finishing all over my body.

As I unwillingly dragged myself home, wearing oversize sunglasses and a baseball cap, I wanted to kill myself, but for real this time. What had I done to myself? I walked block after block in no particular direction, knowing that I would die if I stopped walking or doing something. I couldn't, under any circumstances, be left alone with my thoughts. They were humiliating. The emptiness inside me multiplied at rocket speed. I needed alcohol to fill it back up.

Forty-Seven

I woke up at eight the next morning, hungover as hell. Had there been a day in my life when I'd woken up sober? I was sure there was, but I couldn't recall. I didn't understand why, but my brain had rewired itself, thinking that I needed punishment whenever I was hungover. I didn't think I could endure two hours of sex ever again. But I needed it, for evidently, I'd lost any respect for myself. I had to go to work at noon, but I definitely needed some punishment first.

I sent a message to the misogynist. "*Hey, I can drop by for twenty minutes this afternoon before work.*" I could definitely endure twenty minutes of him. But he failed to reply. It wasn't until midafternoon when he answered.

"*I don't like quickies,*" he said. "*Stop by after work like a real submissive slave.*"

I didn't reply. When the alcohol fumes exited my body, I no longer craved sexual punishment. I just craved more alcohol to cope with the emptiness inside me.

I no longer cared about finding the formula for happiness. I just wanted to fill the void with something, even sadness, just as long as it wasn't emptiness.

In the bathroom at work, I looked in the mirror and could no longer recognize myself. Who was she, and why did she have a devious smile on her lips? Was she the reincarnation of the devil in the flesh?

Absolutely. Good girl gone bad. I'd never realized that was possible for me. But looking back, it made sense, starting with my childhood. Any road I took would lead me to this. A badass bitch who would no longer let people take advantage of her. Fake confidence protected me like a shield from my adversaries. I'd do anything in my power that I needed to do to survive. I'd become God if needed. Anything to get pulled out of the void, as long as I occupied myself with something, anything.

My mood swings had become habitual. One day I'd wake up feeling positive and all, but after a five-mile run, depression would settle in. I'd cook three steaks per day, for breakfast, lunch, and dinner. Thankfully, I wasn't gaining that much weight, but I'd gained some.

In the meantime, I read copious articles about depression, trying to connect with girls who were like me. Time and time again, research showed how social media affected young people, and I wondered if Molly and alcohol had nothing to do with my sadness and anxiety. I could never admit having an addiction to drugs and alcohol, but I could definitely admit having social media addiction. At least then, it wasn't my fault. I was on social media for hours a day, looking at happy girlfriends. Chloe's posts of pasta from Italy, Candace's galas, and Nikita's hot boyfriend. Ugh! They were so annoying.

You know what really helps during depression? Makeovers. And those include new clothes, jewelry, Botox, and lip and cheekbone injections.

Cinnamon loved how I transformed, looking more and more like her. I dyed my hair auburn at Cinnamon's request. "You owe me one for storming off, bitch," she said at the salon, "so try it. It will be a great color on you."

Now we looked alike.

I felt different, Lindsay 2.0, and when Lyon smacked my butt on the way upstairs—visibly intoxicated—I didn't even mind it for some reason. Cinnamon again spent an hour calming him down or whatever they were doing in the locked room upstairs. Nothing mattered anymore. They could be hooking up for all I cared. And I laughed at my own stupidity. Yeah, right. Like Cinnamon would hook up with an old, unattractive guy like Lyon. Lisa would . . . and I burst out laughing, absurd and illogical.

Spending money helped me feel alive, as if life mattered only when cotton, latex, and lacy underwear were concerned. Money helped me be happyish. Yes, beauty cost money, so I opened two more credit cards.

It's a far-fetched theory, but there was a disconnect inside me between me and young, twenty-one-year-old Chardonnay. Both of us shared my body, and where one was young and naive, the other one thought she knew better and hated her life.

My savings diminished because the young Chardonnay punished me for punishing her and having sex with the misogynist. There's a reason she worked at a strip club—she craved independence so that she wouldn't end up with losers like him. She wanted me to be broke the way she was, and she spent thousands of dollars of my money on clothes and jewelry.

A war had begun inside me between the two of them, and the only time they unified was when I took Molly. Spending money helped her travel back in time to her happy place. Five years ago, even if times were rough, optimism flowed freely in her blood. She shared an air mattress, not even an entire room, with Coco from her club. They lived in a basement apartment with rats and cockroaches, drinking cheap chardonnay and eating takeout Chinese food. And they were happy. That's what the young Chardonnay wanted from me.

I learned from the internet that what I experienced was called *depersonalization*, another possible side effect of Molly. I took microdoses occasionally, filling the void and quieting down the young Chardonnay. Afterward, I wanted to see the misogynist, and he was always available.

Perhaps I could learn to live like that.

Part Eight

Ichika

Debts of money are more easily repaid than those of gratitude.

—JAPANESE PROVERB

Forty-Eight

It was mid-August. I went for a run outside on my day off, stretched, and made lunch. At noon, my friend Nikita texted me, saying to call her when I could.

"What's the matter?" I asked when she picked up.

"How's your credit score?"

"Not sure, why?"

"Are you charging stuff to credit cards?"

"I do."

"So Joaquin stole thousands of dollars in cash from the safe and fled to Chile."

"What?"

"I gave him the safe combination because we were getting married in a month."

"How much money are you talking about?"

"Fifty grand, plus another fifty in jewelry."

"Nikita, this is so messed up. Anything I can do?"

"I need money to pay creditors. I'm half a million dollars in debt."

This was news to me. "How come?"

"From the café. I kept on taking out loans to pay for merchandise. Do you have anything to lend?"

"Nikita, I'm broke too."

"Damn! Why didn't I see that one coming? Am I being punished for something? Why does this happen to me?"

"I don't know."

"You really don't have anything? I need to borrow ten grand as soon as possible."

"I've maxed out my credit cards, Nikita. It's a long story and is also not a pretty one. Did you call the police?"

"Of course, but Joaquin is already out of the country."

As we hung up, I sat in the kitchen over a salad, perplexed. While scrolling through Facebook, I noticed how Nikita shared more positive affirmations, and my jaw dropped. Maybe she wasn't as positive a person as I thought, but a fake one who always lived in the first stage of grief: denial. Stranded in a loop. Without an end in sight. Perhaps being negative in the past helped me avoid men like Joaquin stealing thousands of dollars from me.

Forty-Nine

I was home alone. Liam had a shift at the restaurant, Lise had a showing, and Lisa was in Delaware to visit her family. I'd invited Cinnamon for a glass of rosé before

Randy's. I wanted to tell her about the misogynist before I told anyone else, but my plan was interrupted—by Cinnamon herself.

When she walked in, it was like looking in the mirror. She visibly relished in our resemblance, with me following her. Guys had mistaken us for sisters at Randy's, and since we both had no siblings, those comments gave us family bonds.

As we assembled in the living room with two glasses of wine, Cinnamon whispered, "Are your roommates home?"

"No," I said.

"That's too bad. I really wanted to meet Lisa. I wanna see what the old bag looks like."

"She has a bunch of framed pictures in her bedroom."

"Can I see?"

"Of course."

Lisa had mentioned she didn't mind if I went into her room to grab something. Typically, it involved self-help books.

When Cinnamon entered Lisa's room, she asked, "Is this the master?"

"Yes."

"Huge."

Lisa had a king-size bed in the middle of the bedroom with black sateen sheets, the bed perfectly made and pillows fluffed. Lisa's love for black appeared in her choice of rugs, furniture, and wardrobe.

Cinnamon opened the closet, to my shrieking.

"Cinnamon, don't!"

"Relax. I just wanna take a look."

"What if she has cameras installed to make sure nobody is spying on her?"

"Chardonnay, seriously. Nobody installs cameras in their closets because they're afraid of getting spied on. Have you ever looked at how much cameras cost? Lisa's wardrobe is so boring, by the way."

"Just like her personality," I said.

"Let's see what other secrets she has."

"Cinnamon, please don't. Let's return to the living room."

Cinnamon ignored me and opened the first drawer of Lisa's dresser that stood against the wall opposite her bed.

"Ooh la la," she sang. "Cool glasses."

She put on Lisa's sunglasses and turned, modeling them for me. "Hi, I'm Lisa, the bitch of the house."

I laughed and said, "Put them back."

Instead, Cinnamon opened the second drawer, then the third, and closed them just as fast. In the bottom drawer, she saw something that she liked.

"This should be interesting," she said while I stood in the doorway, listening for the sound of keys. If Lise returned from her showing and caught us snooping, I'd be doomed.

"Cinnamon, hurry up," I said, looking behind my shoulder.

She closed the bottom drawer with the bottom of her heel and said, "OK, I'm done."

I sat down on the couch, relieved, while Cinnamon positioned herself in a rocking chair across from me.

"How much does Lisa pay for rent, by the way?" she asked, then took a sip of rosé.

"I don't know."

"How much do you pay, Chardonnay?"

"I pay six hundred."

"And how much for the entire apartment?"

"I don't know, Cinnamon. I never asked. Why?"

"Do you know how much the faggot pays?"

"He's not a faggot. Seriously, can you not say things like that?"

"Fine, Chardonnay. Ugh. The gay guy—how much does he pay?"

"Liam said he pays eight hundred, but his room is bigger than mine. I made some calculations just for fun, and I think Lisa pays over four thousand for the whole place."

"I don't think so, Chardonnay. I think the old hag takes advantage of you. Just the size of her room alone is bigger than my studio on Twenty-First Street. She overcharges you . . . I promise."

"I don't think so. Lise with an *e* is the real estate agent, and she's a nice one. She wouldn't let Lisa with an *a* take advantage of me."

"Chardonnay, I love you, but you sound just like Aspen, girl. This is New York, and people take advantage of everyone. I told you that before on the train to Asbury Park. Do you remember working at Cookie's strip club? Don't you think Cookie took advantage of us by having old dickheads touch us for money? Don't tell me it's because we agreed to it. Sure, we did, but did we know any better? Adults are the ones who should know better and prohibit young girls from engaging in such atrocious activities."

"What are you saying?"

"I'm saying everyone takes advantage of everyone in this damn town, and your roommates take advantage of you whether you like it or not."

"Cinnamon, you sound angry."

"I'm angry because the old hag makes money off you."

"How do you know that?"

"Well, that's fucking how!" she said and showed me her phone.

"What's that?" I asked.

"Take a closer look, dear fool. I found the lease for your apartment and took a picture of it."

"Oh my God. You found the lease?"

"Well, read what the total rent is, Chardonnay."

I took her phone in my hands. "Where is it? I can't find it."

"Read number three. The total rent is . . ." she stretched out the last word, waiting for my answer.

"Oh my God," I said. "It says the total rent is nineteen hundred."

"Which makes Lisa and Lise pay, what?"

"I'm not good at math, Cinnamon."

"The two of them pay five hundred dollars. That's two-fifty each—per month."

"I don't believe it."

"I know you're in shock and in denial, but I told you many times that people in this town are disgusting. Starting with bitches like Cookie, who deserves to rot inside Rikers."

"But . . . I mean . . . I agreed to six hundred, didn't I?"

"That's not how it works. Just because you agree to something, it doesn't automatically make it OK. When you don't know any better, you're the gullible one. And assholes like Lisa take advantage of people like you and Aspen. If not for me, Aspen would still live with two Orientals who robbed her blind."

"Cinnamon! Orientals? Faggots? Really? That's inappropriate."

"Oh, you care about what's appropriate? Then play by the rules and get taken advantage of by Lisa and the rest of the world."

"Why are you getting upset?"

"Because, Chardonnay, you're annoying. I found Aspen a much better place with *white* girls who know struggle, not some rich, privileged Orientals whose daddies leased a three-bedroom while they attended NYU. I won't let Lisas and Cookies get away with this."

"What, are you going to kill them all?"

"I would if I could. Doesn't that make you angry?"

"Yes, but I don't know what I can do."

"Well, you agreed to pay six hundred, so there's nothing you can do, except either continue contributing to their wealth or confront the old hag."

"I can't confront her, Cinnamon. I'm not supposed to paw through her dresser."

"She's probably pawed through yours."

"Let's go to Randy's and I'll think about it," I said, finishing my rosé.

Fifty

The end of August brought even worse news. Work had been busy with back-to-school sales, and the four of us worked at the store on most days. To cope with our misery, Aspen, Cinnamon, and I frequented Randy's every night. You could set your clock by watching us.

Once a week, I allowed myself a higher dose of Molly and spent the next day with the misogynist, tied up in his bed. It had become so routine, I quite literally craved it. I couldn't wait for Fridays. He was the only person who knew I took Molly, and he loved it. Molly made me submissive. He couldn't believe how open I was to trying new things, as, quote, "Other girls are such prudes. Dinner, movie, dating. You're a special girl."

I loved being special to him—to anyone, really.

I tried avoiding Lisa as much as possible, afraid I might say something mean. I was uncertain what to do about the rent. I even browsed online, but nothing was cheaper. So technically, my rent was still a good deal. Plus, I couldn't believe how disgustingly other girls lived. From pictures alone, some had filthy apartments, mismatched furniture, and tiny bedrooms. And yet, they asked for $700 or more. Cheaper and nicer apartments obviously existed, but Woodside and Sunnyside were the closest, with a longer commute.

I realized the four cornerstones of happiness had changed for me. And while I no longer felt happy and naive as an optimist, I was happy and content as a realist. Perhaps there was a distinction, levels of happiness I'd failed to understand before.

Nobody I knew had a perfect life. Drinking, gambling, cheating ... something was involved to some degree. At least I was honest with myself and content in knowing that while I'd never become who I'd been before—a happy-go-lucky Lindsay—I needed to persevere in the present.

On the other hand, luck and happiness appeared to follow my friends anywhere they went.

Chloe loved traveling, or so it seemed from her posts. The best part was that she no longer sent me angry messages. I guess when we're happy and occupy our time with what we love, anger no longer guides us.

Nikita learned she was pregnant, but it wasn't Joaquin's—it was Juan's, a guy from her restaurant, a rebound and a new boyfriend. She'd applied for bankruptcy and decided to keep the baby. I was shocked. Nothing could bring Nikita down, and I simultaneously admired her and was scared for her well-being.

Candace found a good surgeon who could turn her into a woman, but it would cost $25,000, an amount of money she didn't yet have. Candace was still in limbo and said, "I can't wait until I have the money in my hands; only then will I be happy."

As for me, a bump on the road awaited too. On August thirtieth, in the afternoon, while I worked at Lyon's, Lisa sent me a text message:

Don't freak out, but Liam found bedbugs in his bedroom and in the living room. We must exterminate as soon as possible—tomorrow—said the landlord. The company rep said we must wash all our clothes in hot water and dry them for two hours on high heat, then tie them tightly in plastic bags—we must do it today. Also, we must stay somewhere for two days because the chemicals they use are strong. Like, I didn't realize how many bedbugs we had, and they multiply quickly. Do you know someone you can stay with or get a hotel for two nights?

Aspen approached me as I finished reading the text and said, "You're so pale, girl. Are you OK?"

"I don't know," I said and showed her the text.

"Oh my God," she said, then threw my phone at me, as if it had the bugs. "Ew, bedbugs."

"What is the matter now, Aspen?" asked Cinnamon.

She stood behind us, and Aspen jumped, saying, "Oh gosh, you scared me. Lindsay has bedbugs."

"Really?" Cinnamon asked me and wrinkled her nose in disgust.

"Yes," I said and showed her Lisa's text.

"What will you do?" Aspen asked me. "Bedbugs are like crabs for adults. So embarrassing."

"Aspen, shut the fuck up," Cinnamon said. "We live in Astoria, and bedbugs are not embarrassing. It's not like they're Lindsay's fault."

"I haven't even thought about it or processed the information," I said. "You think my roommates will blame me?"

"Why you?" Cinnamon asked.

"Because I'm the new roommate, and now all of a sudden we have bedbugs."

"You have bedbug?" asked Ichika.

The three of us turned and found Ichika behind us eating sunflower seeds.

"Yes, she does," Cinnamon said. "And she needs to stay somewhere for two days."

I was absolutely certain Cinnamon would invite me to stay at her studio, and I'd refuse obligatorily even if I wanted to stay with her. Instead, Cinnamon said, "Aspen, Lindsay will stay with you."

"I wish," Aspen said, "but my roommates don't allow people to just stay with us. I live with two girls. And we have a strict no-visitors policy. She could stay with you, though."

"Oh, Lindsay, I wish, but, I'm, um, actually," Cinnamon said, at a loss for words.

The phone rang, and Cinnamon raced to pick it up.

"You stay with me, Mizumi," Ichika said.

"With you?" I said.

Aspen cringed but said nothing.

"I have couch, but no pillow. You bring," Ichika said.

"Ichika, I don't feel comfortable staying with you. I have friends in Astoria I could stay with."

That was a lie, but what she didn't know wouldn't hurt her. I planned on staying at a hotel, wondering how much that would cost me. In the past month alone, I'd purchased an entirely new wardrobe, spending $5,000 from my cash stash. I thought it was a smart investment with the salary coming in (even if Cinnamon received my commissions for my Asbury Park outburst). How long the payouts would last, she hadn't specified.

"OK," Ichika said, "you stay with friend."

I sat at the desk, watching the store spin around me, becoming a haze of blurry shapes. I hated Aspen and Cinnamon right now, even if I understood why they didn't want me to stay with them. I felt like a diseased whore with Ebola, SARS, and hepatitis, whom everyone tried to avoid.

Flashbacks from high school flickered when I overheard girls talking about me: "Lindsay lives with foster parents, and my mom told me to stay away from her." Or, "Those kids come from disruptive families. Alcoholics, drug addicts." Or, "Can you believe she actually wants to audition to be a cheerleader?"

Bedbugs couldn't have come at a worse time. That was quite literally the last problem I needed to deal with then. The void inside me kept multiplying faster than the universe in my shaken mental space, eating me from the inside out. Kids used to call me skin and bone, and that's who I became again, with nothing inside me.

Almost on the verge of tears, I found Ichika upstairs.

I said, "I'll stay with you if that's OK."

"OK, Mizumi. But I no have extra pillow. You bring from our store. Pick one upstair."

Fifty-One

The worst part about having bedbugs has nothing to do with the actual bedbugs. The worst part is washing everything you own. I ended up having twenty trash bags full of clothes, all washed and dried on high heat. I'd taken the rest of the afternoon off to make it happen. Trash bags were suggested by the exterminator. Then you can just throw the bags out.

Ichika lived in Flushing, which some people call the Chinatown of Queens. I'd never been there before, simply because Flushing was the last stop on the 7 Line, and I assumed it would take about two hours by train. Ichika picked me up in the evening after she finished work. Her car was an old, beat-up Prius in an unnaturally bright yellow color.

"You bring pillow?" she asked as soon as I opened the passenger door.

"It's in one of my bags," I said, then put my bags on the back seat. "I bought one from Cinnamon. Gave her a commission."

We reached Flushing in fifteen minutes via a highway route. I assumed Ichika would be driving like an old lady, but she played pop music and drove over the speed limit of fifty-five.

"Before home, we stop at store for food. OK, Mizumi?" she said as she parallel-parked on Kissena Boulevard.

The grocery store was something I'd never seen before. There were rows of oversize vegetables—like a zucchini that was six feet long—followed by live turtles, eels, and crabs. If Ichika made me a turtle for dinner, I'd flee to a nearby motel. Fortunately for me, she picked up a bunch of fresh produce and tea, and we proceeded to the checkout.

Her apartment complex stood across the street, a tall, reddish building the color of my Cinnamon-inspired hair. Dusk had painted the sky opaque blue, suggesting an imminent sunset. I picked up my bags from the car while we chatted about nothing in particular. Sometimes I couldn't even understand her but nodded as if I did.

An Asian doorman greeted us downstairs, and the two exchanged foreign words—maybe Japanese? I wasn't sure. The two of us took an elevator to the twentieth floor and exited to a hallway carpeted in beige.

"Twenty, *em*," Ichika said.

"What's that?"

"My house. *Em*, like *Mizumi*."

I had a hard time understanding her mumbling, and Ichika laughed until we approached apartment 20-M.

"Oh," was all I said. M like *Mizumi*.

When Ichika opened the door, straight across, I saw Manhattan through her windows.

"Shoe off, Mizumi," she said, taking off her flats.

The apartment was small but neat, barely any furniture. Hardwood floors, tall palms in every corner.

"I love plant," she said, watching my facial expressions. "Ichika: one thousand flower."

"They're beautiful," I said.

"Come. I show."

She walked me through the apartment, narrating, "This is bedroom."

"Where is the bed?"

"No bed. I sleep on floor."

Ichika approached an ornamental chiffonier, lacquered cherrywood, and opened a drawer. She pulled out a yoga mat and what resembled a foam roller.

"My bed, my pillow," she said about the two items.

The bathroom was small, with a shower but no bath. The living room and kitchen were the same room, separated by a couch, gray and modern. With the employee discount, I expected her to have leather furniture from Lyon's, but clearly, her taste differed in a better way.

"You don't have anything from our store," I noted.

"No," she said. "Leather is bad for animal. Ugly too."

"I agree," I said and started giggling.

"Why laugh?"

"It's hilarious that we all hate the furniture we sell, and yet we're there every day, selling it like it's the best thing on Earth."

"No matter what we think. Other people like. Lyon know what people buy. Ugly leather."

"How long have you worked for Lyon?"

"Oh, many year. Sometime I think I work a month. Other day, I think I work twenty year. Hard to say."

"Do you have any wine, by any chance?"

"No, I no drink. Asian culture, drink is bad. We have no bar in Flushing."

"Wait, for real?" I asked, surprised.

"One Irish bar on corner, but no more bar."

I was so struck by surprise, I instantly looked it up on my phone. Ichika was right. While in Astoria, 70 percent of businesses were bars, only one bar appeared in the entire Flushing.

"I make noodle for dinner," she said. "You sit and relax. OK, Mizumi?"

While Ichika was busy cooking, Cinnamon texted me: *"How's the crazy? Have you found any corpses yet?"*

"Surprisingly neat. She doesn't have a bed."

"Where does she sleep?"

"On a yoga mat and a muscle roller."

"Send me a picture. I want to show Aspen. What is she doing now?"

"Cooking."

"Oh Lord. You will be full of MSG by morning."

"Mizumi," Ichika yelled from the kitchen. "Dinner ready."

I approached the dining table, which was wooden and round. I sat down, watching Ichika hustle over the kitchen counter, where she filled up two bowls.

"I make shrimp noodle," she said. "I love shrimp."

"Me too."

She placed the bowls on the table next to various condiments. Soy sauce, red chili paste, chopped garlic, fresh cilantro.

"You add what you like, Mizumi."

"I like everything as long as it's not too spicy."

"Then no take chili paste."

I added the condiments and tasted the broth by sipping from the bowl.

"You like?" she asked.

"It tastes incredible, Ichika."

"Thank you."

When she started eating with chopsticks, I realized I didn't know how.

"Do you have a fork?" I asked.

"Fork?" she asked. "I think."

She ventured back to the kitchen, opening cabinets.

"I find one," she said. It was a plastic fork and knife kit from a takeout order.

In the middle of the dinner, she asked, "Why you friend with Cinnamon? You so differ."

"We've known each other for years."

"Lyon hate Cinnamon."

"He does?"

"She unkind. Late for work. Always text on phone. Selfie."

"If he hates Cinnamon, why hasn't he fired her? There are so many people he could find as a replacement."

"I think it hard to replace. We do thing we hate, but we still do. Why? Nobody know."

"I agree," I said, and while thinking about my love-hate relationship with the misogynist, alcohol, and Molly, my cheeks heated up.

"I miss Japan," she said. "But my life ... better here."

"Do you ever go back to visit?"

"No. My parent die. I only child."

"Me too. I don't have any siblings."

"What about your parent?"

"I was abandoned in a hospital," I said, and all of a sudden, a tear appeared, followed by more. "I'm sorry, Ichika. I didn't mean to cry. Your question was just so unexpected, and with these bedbugs, I can't control myself."

Ichika stood up and hugged me while I let the tears flow. I never cried in front of people and felt embarrassed.

Ichika asked no more questions. She cleaned up after dinner, took a shower, and said good night.

While on the couch, nestled under a blanket, I scrolled through social media on my phone. I realized that today was the first time in a decade someone made me dinner at home. I didn't know what to do with that realization. Did I deserve it? I didn't think so. Well, the *young* Chardonnay believed I didn't deserve it. It seemed unfair that while she had no one taking care of her, Ichika took care of me—as if I were a better person. I had no drugs or alcohol to quiet the young Chardonnay down, and as I remained on the couch, I thought about the misogynist.

For the next two hours, we exchanged dirty texts back and forth. He made me go to the bathroom and take naked pictures, and in return, he sent me his.

"You'll soon be riding this," he said. *"What if we invited two buddies of mine?"*

"Like a foursome?"

"Yeah."

"I've never done one before."

"It's fun. You'll love it."

He followed with a picture of two of his friends, both young, handsome gym rats like himself, who evidently enjoyed punishing girls in bed.

"I'll think about it," I said.

"There's nothing to think about. Take Molly and come over tomorrow."

And that's exactly what I did the following afternoon on my day off.

Fifty-Three

Suffice it to say, the young Chardonnay was satisfied, but I hated myself more and more. The three of them took turns with me, and on the way to Ichika's by taxi, I felt so empty inside that I thought of killing myself again.

In the taxi, street numbers increased while my self-esteem proportionally decreased. That feeling had become so normal, I realized it no longer had the same effect as before. I used that term in a different context—by *killing myself,* I meant I actually wanted to punish myself. I wanted to suffer more. I'm not sure how to explain it any better.

The concept of crime and punishment had been so engraved inside of me that as soon as I got to Ichika's, I poured myself a glass of wine to calm myself down. I felt sorry for myself, then laughed at the stupidity of that sentiment. I craved punishment; then I craved punishment for punishing myself while feeling sorry for myself. My boyfriend—if that's what you'd call him—was sharing me with his friends. Soon enough, foursomes would be as normal as being tied up. Would I ever hit my limit of humiliation and degradation? Or was I as limitless as the universe? I'd normalized everything from alcohol to drugs to dirty sex.

I had no boundaries anymore. And without boundaries, who was I at all? Without boundaries and principles, I was a slave pushed around by men and women. While Lisa took advantage of me rent-wise, Cinnamon had sucked out all of my soul. The misogynist would text me, and I would stand on his doorstep, ready for orders.

I was spiraling down. I knew I would eventually hit my rock bottom. Fall hard and break apart. After all, I was nothing but a bottle of Chardonnay, and I would shatter into a million pieces.

Fifty-Four

Ichika made salmon teriyaki with jasmine rice for dinner. I had no idea she was such a good cook. Plus, she munched on all these carbs and yet remained rail-thin, whereas my tummy started to grow slowly in the direction of the sun.

After dinner, Lisa sent me another long text. "*So the exterminator said your mattress was so infested with bedbugs, they had to throw it out. That cost extra. They said we had bedbugs to begin with because of the mattress you bought at your store. Altogether, it came to six hundred dollars. So for September, your rent is a thousand and two hundred, hunny.*"

Hunny? What a freaking bitch. I couldn't believe my eyes, so I typed: "*How did they know the bedbugs came from my mattress?*"

"*It was the biggest infestation. Lise, Liam, and I, we have mattress protectors. But you didn't have one. Lise said you could borrow her air mattress again.*"

I no longer had access to my body, and something I can only describe as rage filled me as I typed: "*How about I pay the entire rent? How much is it, by the way? Nineteen hundred, you say? Great. Six hundred for me, eight hundred for Liam, and five hundred for you and Lise. Plus, six hundred for the exterminator. How funny that the sum is always so nice and round. Like your stupid, bloated face.*"

When Lisa failed to reply, my rage continued. "*Oh yes. I know everything. How you take advantage of us. You big fat liar.*"

Lisa didn't deny the truth but replied: "*I didn't take advantage of anyone. You agreed to six hundred. Why do you have a problem with it now? And for future reference, please do not go through my stuff. Thanks.*"

Part Nine

The Formula For Happiness

Happiness is when what you think, what you say, and what you do are in harmony.

—MAHATMA GANDHI

Fifty-Five

I lay on Ichika's couch in the dark, thinking that perhaps Japanese people had been right all along about one thing. Four is indeed an unlucky number, be it a four-bedroom apartment or a foursome. What also was wrong: the four of us working at Lyon's.

The following day, suicidal thoughts, also known as post-Molly aftermath, were made worse by Cinnamon avoiding me as if I carried bedbugs in my purse. I felt lonely, friendless, and ignored, the worst combination. I'd alienated myself and ruined my relationship with my roommates, and Aspen and Cinnamon avoided me like the plague. I was on the second floor by myself, looking out the window. The tree growing outside couldn't stand still, and as the wind buffeted its branches, they leaned back and forth as if doing yoga. I couldn't remember the last time I did yoga.

When Cinnamon entered my life, she pushed anything remotely spiritual out of me. Like a disease, she spread toxicity through my veins, made me fall in love with her on Molly, and ruined my relationship with Lisa and Lise.

Cinnamon texted me: *"Lyon is high as a kite. He just walked in. Don't talk to him."*

I felt snarky because I wanted to punish Cinnamon for treating me like an animal. *"So?"* I texted back.

"Are you OK? You seemed weird today."

"I'm mad because you're avoiding me."

"Chardonnay, you have bedbugs at home. There's nothing wrong with being careful on my part."

"The bedbugs came from the store!"

"No, they didn't, Chardonnay. Stop listening to your stupid roommate, or you'll end up like her."

"Stop listening to her and start listening to you?"

I no longer felt like myself. I hadn't in weeks, in fact. I used to be that happy-go-lucky girl with dreams and aspirations, and today I'd woken up a girl who envisioned her own death. I laughed at the morbidity of my pathetic thoughts, a reflection of my pathetic self. I went up to the fourth floor, where we had another bathroom, and locked myself in. I was panicking and needed a quick fix. Thankfully, I had plenty of cocaine left that I'd purchased from Cinnamon for "Liam."

When I floated up in the sky, I looked at myself staring into the bathroom mirror, a formerly pretty girl with clear skin and toned abs. I could no longer recognize myself in the mirror. I had changed mentally, and that change mirrored my physical appearance—auburn hair, fillers, six-inch rose-pink heels. I looked at my fingers. When had I purchased a diamond ring from Tiffany's? What about the pendant necklace in white gold with a *C* for Chardonnay? Or did the *C* stand for Cinnamon?

How much money had I spent on cocaine and Molly?

I don't remember exiting the bathroom, but I bumped into Lyon when I did. And that's when I saw his face, high and bloated, akin to mine.

"Just the girl I wanted to talk to," he said. "Come with me, Cinnamon."

He grabbed my arm before I could protest and tell him I was Chardonnay. Then I forgot what I wanted to say. A blank.

Lyon took me inside his office, the locked door with the STAFF ONLY sign next to the bathroom. I'd never been inside it—the office where I twice heard him moan from crying—and my body had become stiff and reluctant. The last thing I needed was Lyon crying his problems to me, thinking I was Cinnamon while high on drugs.

Two TV monitors showed the store in real time, each screen split onto four screens. Cinnamon sat downstairs at the desk, texting on her phone. A customer roamed around the third floor. Two empty bathrooms.

"Kick my balls," Lyon said.

"What?" I asked.

"I said kick my balls, Cinnamon."

"I'm not Cinnamon."

His eyes found mine, one by one. "What are you talking about?"

"I'm not Cinnamon," I said. "I'm Chardonnay, Lyon."

"I said *kick my balls*. Now!"

I reached for the door, but he covered it with his body. He was sweating profusely, forehead damp and wrinkly, his eyes scurrying and enflamed. Belatedly, I noticed he wore an orange polo shirt with cargo shorts and loafers.

"Lyon, please don't," I said. Fear had pinched my stomach, my throat tight. I'd discovered a sexual fetish of his, and he could kill me if the secret was released.

"I saw what you do in the bathroom, Cinnamon, you cocaine-snorting slut."

"I'm not Cinnamon!"

"Why are you one and the same? Don't matter. I gave you a job, and now you give me what I want. Kick me in my nuts, and nobody knows what you look like when you snort snow."

He spread his feet to shoulder-width and closed his eyes.

"Lyon, I can't do this."

"Kick mine or I'll kick yours."

"It's not legal to film in the bathroom, Lyon."

"Just kick my nuts and I'll pay you."

Without waiting for a response, Lyon reached inside a pocket in his cargo shorts, pulling out his wallet. Dollar bills rustled as he took them out, a mix of twenties and fifties, and gave them to me.

"Lyon, I'm not going to have sex for money."

"Just kick my balls. No sex."

Lyon unbuckled his belt and pulled his shorts down, followed by green, shiny boxers. I couldn't see his genitalia, as his stomach hid it; no hair anywhere, smooth all over. I took the money, closed my eyes, and kicked him in his groin.

"Harder," he said, moaning.

Am I Cookie now? I asked myself as I kicked him again and again until he groaned ... again, and he wailed ... again, and he started crying from pain or pleasure, the same feeling for him—intertwined in the brain.

"Blab to anyone and you're dead," he said. "I know people."

Somehow, I knew that much was true. He let me exit the room, my hands shaking and my throat so tense I thought I'd suffocate. There was a total of $180 in my hands, the price for kicking Lyon in the nuts. Was I now officially a prostitute, or did it not count because there was no consent? People in power can get away with a million things, and rape is one of them.

Could I trust Cinnamon if I told her what had just happened? She obviously knew about his fetishes, about everything. She'd kicked his balls before and had recruited me, fresh meat, so Lyon could take advantage of me.

Who was I? Lindsay? Or was I Cinnamon, Chardonnay, or Cookie? Why did it feel like my life happened parallel to me rather than happening to me? I had lost my will to live, lost my friends, and now I'd lost any—if I ever had it—respect for myself. There had once been an innocence about Lindsay that no longer gushed in my veins.

As I walked down the stairs, I promised myself never to return, frightened of Lyon and what could happen to me if I ever told anyone the truth. I'd met people like him at Cookie's club—rich, smart, and arrogant—men who had everything and had no respect for anyone else.

I wondered if I could call Lucy Brownstein and beg to have my live-in nanny job back—kick out whichever new girl worked there now. I was allowed to return to my apartment now that the extermination was over, but I wanted to never have to live there again with Lisa and Lise. I wanted to disappear.

Disappear . . . the story of my life.

Running away has always helped me avoid unnecessary awkwardness. I hate goodbyes and apologies, and running away helps accomplish both so effortlessly in one single step.

The only world I saw myself in at that moment was Randy's.

As I took a seat at Randy's, I raised my hand, getting the bartender's attention. Two other patrons went about their drinking business on the other side of the bar.

While the bartender mixed my drink, I texted Cinnamon and asked her to meet me at Randy's.

"What for?"

"We need to talk."

"I'm busy tonight, Chardonnay."

"I kicked Lyon in the balls."

"Don't say another word. I'll meet you at Randy's as soon as I can close the store."

By the time Cinnamon entered Randy's, I was high and drunk. "Sweet Dreams" by the Eurhythmics played too loudly for her taste, and I heard her telling the bartender, "Turn it down, OK?"

He did as told until he received Cinnamon's thumbs-up. She'd been controlling everyone in this neighborhood, I realized. From Lyon's to Randy's and all the people in between. Her demeanor had changed from friendly to coldhearted, and I hated her. I hated everything about her right now.

"Chardonnay, what happened?" she asked me as she took a sip of her martini, a yellow lemon drop.

"Lyon took advantage of me. He locked me in the room upstairs. There are monitors with cameras in every corner of the store, even in the bathroom."

"That sick cocksucker."

"Ha!"

"Ha, what?"

"You know everything."

"I know we have cameras. I didn't know they were in every bathroom."

"Bullshit, Cinnamon. You've always lied to me. The very first night you hooked me on Molly, which I've been taking since, I knew you were a lying asshole—like Lisa."

"Chardonnay, you're drunk. Go home and call me when you're sober."

"Cinnamon doesn't enjoy hearing criticisms. What a surprise! Ha!"

"You're an adult, Chardonnay, and if you took Molly without my supervision, that's on you."

"That's what you said about Cookie. That she should be blamed for recruiting girls. Why doesn't that apply to you?"

"Because I don't recruit anyone, and I meant very young girls, eighteen, nineteen. You're a grown-up, Chardonnay, and if you blame me for your addiction, then fuck you."

"That's not a thing a friend would say."

"It *is* a thing a friend would say, Chardonnay, because I've just said it, and I think you need to lay off alcohol for a while."

"You're the one who introduced me to this bar."

"That doesn't mean I want you to become an alcoholic."

"I had friends with whom I did other things aside from drinking and getting high—like shopping and watching movies. With you and Aspen, there's nothing but constant gossiping, shoplifting, and three-way phone calls about nothing."

"You're blaming me for that, girl?"

"Someone must be blamed."

"Then blame yourself. I don't need your shit, Chardonnay. So you did *one* thing for your boss. Was it really that bad to take out your own anger on someone so pathetic?"

"That *bad*? He basically raped me."

"Don't be so dramatic. He was high on cocaine, and he won't even remember that it happened. Maybe you just misunderstood him because you were high yourself."

"In fact, Lyon thought I was you, and that's why he took me to the room and asked me to *kick him in the balls*!"

"Don't shout. Alcohol and drugs do that to unstable people—make them see and hear things."

"You're telling me I'm unstable?"

"Look at yourself, Chardonnay. Look what has become of you. You're snappy and insecure, and you blame everyone."

"Would it be better if I followed Kitty and died?"

"Stop being so dramatic. I won't tolerate your adolescent outbursts just because you did something out of your comfort zone. That has nothing to do with me."

"I don't work there anymore."

"I really don't care right now," she said. "You're not on the books, and you're free to go whenever."

"How can you say that, Cinnamon?"

"You just said you wanted to quit. So quit."

"But how can you *say* that? You don't care about anyone but yourself."

"I take care of myself and advise you to do the same."

"Cinnamon, I had savings before I started working there, and now I'm in debt. All because of you."

"What are you talking about?"

"I never bought drugs for Liam. They were for me."

"And you blame me, Chardonnay? You're the liar around here. Don't be mad at me."

"I'm in debt because I've changed. I don't know who I am anymore. Look at this freaking ring." I flung my hand in her face and continued, "It cost me five thousand dollars, and I don't recall buying it. Now Lisa wants me to pay for the stupid exterminator. And if I don't have a job, I don't know how I'll pay for everything."

"Nobody is firing you, Chardonnay."

"So I should stay and kick Lyon in the nuts on an ongoing basis when he's high on cocaine? Is that my life right now? Is that what you suggest?"

"Sober up, Chardonnay. That's what I suggest."

"You're just a bitch. You've always been. You don't care about anyone but yourself."

"I'm a bitch? I gave you that job to begin with, and I told you Lisa took advantage of you. I took you back after you stole my wine at Asbury Park, acting like a lunatic."

"I was not myself. You should've warned me about the side effects of Molly—a personality disorder."

"I forgave you for everything, and this is how you repay me, by blaming me?"

"I'm not the one with a baby bump, stealing clothes at Bloomingdale's."

"Oh, fuck both of your faces, Chardonnay. So the day when you receive a free dress is fine, but when you're infuriated, I'm a shoplifter and a scapegoat for your dilemmas? You're a two-faced, fake tramp, and I never wanna see your laughable mug ever again. You understand? In fact, if you don't leave, I'll claw your eyes out."

I stood up from my seat. "I knew it. Upon getting accused of being called a fake friend, you show your true colors and call me two-faced—reversing the tables. Classic Cinnamon."

Cinnamon grabbed my hair from behind and pulled it. I screamed. The bartender rushed to the middle like a referee, and Cinnamon let go.

"No fighting here," he said. "Go outside."

"She's leaving," Cinnamon told him, then turned to me. "Go home to your stupid roommates, you stupid drug addict."

I made it outside, operating on autopilot through the crowded streets, block after block, until I reached my corner. My former mattress, wrapped in a clear plastic bag, rested on the ground. My hands shook as I wrestled with my purse, trying to find my keys. I found the nutmeg that Lise had gifted me and threw it toward the darkness of the street. She said it was for good luck. Ha!

Anger had made me disoriented, but I took a breath and focused on finding the keys. I found them at the bottom, entered the building, and climbed to the second floor. The chemical odor, a reminder of the recent extermination, was strong. I almost saw it as a cloud. Inside, the apartment was a mess—black trash bags filled with clothes everywhere—and no longer could my legs uphold my body's weight. I slid down, cold hardwood floor against my skin.

Texts began pouring in, one after another. Cinnamon, Cinnamon, Cinnamon. I wanted to break the phone against the wall, but I knew I'd regret it.

I needed a stronger high, yet I feared Molly would make matters worse, tipping my neurotransmitters out of calibration. A bag of Molly was calling my name ... hidden behind the painting in my room. I tasted tears, salty and freeing, and stood up.

I dropped half a bag of Molly on my tongue, equaling a dose and a half. The bitter white powder stung, chemical and unnatural. I ran to the kitchen for some water. Lisa and Lise were in the living room, and they watched me without saying a word.

Back in my bedroom, I texted the misogynist, asking him whether I could spend the night at his place. I added that I was on Molly, so there was something in it for him—a helpless girl, the way he likes it. Lise's air mattress rested in the corner by my air conditioner, my room hot and stuffy. The extermination chemicals had left a sheen along the baseboards, trash bags all over. Mess. My life was a mess.

"Sweet Dreams" from Randy's was stuck in my head. I find it fascinating how certain songs can evoke memories and can even become physical. Several times while working at Lyon's, if I heard a song that I normally listened to while running, I would start sweating as if I were actually running. Sounds, smells, and tastes can act similarly, reminding us of critical events in our lives. Even if you only hear thunder once in your life, you'll recognize it the next time. Celery juice still reminds me of those days when barfing was my only option to remain in shape. Cumin takes me back to the foster family in Kissimmee, Florida, the father's hand touching parts of me prohibited by law.

The misogynist texted back, *"My girlfriend is in town this week. I'll text you when she leaves."*

He had a girlfriend?

Then who was I?

I wanted to run away, disappear far away in the jungle where nobody could ever find me. The young Chardonnay had achieved exactly what she wanted. I was single, penniless, and mentally unstable, unsure how I'd managed to spend my savings on clothes and accessories, all of which were tied up in trash bags scattered around my bedroom. Drinks, drugs, and diamonds had drained my cash, and I'd hit a limit on my credit cards, owing over $10,000.

Akin to Ichika, I'd been planting roasted sunflower seeds all over the place, hopelessly expecting yellow flowers in return. One of them was my friendship with Cinnamon, with its highly unlikely and improbable success rate. We were nothing alike. Cinnamon needed someone agreeable like Aspen, and I'd become argumentative.

My other roasted sunflower seed was falling in love with the misogynist by route of the classic Stockholm syndrome. I expected to be discarded at the end, a broken toy whose value diminished more each time she was used.

Why did I keep punishing myself by choosing the wrong paths when signs clearly pointed in the opposite direction?

Because that was my greatest strength: I was great at self-sabotage.

Such a realization brought me happiness for some twisted reason. Deep inside, I craved love, friendship, and affection, but the young Chardonnay inside me didn't believe she was worth it. I found Molly appealing because it helped me quiet her down, and I felt love and affection, even if for a brief moment. I was forced to understand who the young Chardonnay was. I barely remembered her, an impulsive child who was now destroying my future. She was me, and I was her. We were one and the same. Then how come it felt like Chardonnay stood on the other side of the Hudson River, burning the bridge between us? She craved total separation from me because she loathed me, the adult who lived the life she'd wanted.

Who are you, Chardonnay? What do you want?

The two of us had separated—we had disconnected; we had become strangers. She still worked at Cookie's strip club, giving lap dances, and I worked at Lyon's, hitting my boss in the balls. We had two rather different desires, and our separation felt palpable. There were now two of us.

But her happiness and mine should have been one and the same.

For the longest time, I believed that wisdom comes with experience and that time heals all wounds. But as I looked around my bedroom, a life full of trash bags and chemicals, I no longer believed in anything.

I wanted to visit Cookie. She would remind me who Chardonnay was and what she wanted. Cookie hired us, and I knew she must remember.

I envisioned Cookie behind bars after we hadn't spoken in five years. She'd be excited to see us, Lindsay and Chardonnay, together, inseparable like the earth and the moon and exactly that far away from each other. Cookie could provide us with words of advice and wisdom. Five years ago, she was the closest person to being a mom for me.

Suddenly, I was rolling on Molly, rave music blasting from my earphones. I kept looking in the mirror to make sure I was who I thought I was. Every song sounded amazing. Molly sobered me up, just as it did the previous times. Another magical effect of that drug, I guess. I realized I still had friends, my true friends. I called Chloe to tell her how much I loved her and to apologize for offering the nanny job to Kitty. Jealousy had made me do it, and now I understood how unfairly I treated her. Just because Chloe lived with her mother was not an excuse to lash out at a friend of mine. But Chloe was in Italy and didn't pick up.

Weird thoughts raced through my mind, and I began scribbling them down.

I want to sleep, but I want to dance. My teeth feel tight, and I go to the bathroom every two minutes. I miss all of my friends, and yet I never reach out to them. I'm bloated as hell, and I keep drinking lots of coconut water to replenish electrolytes. My friends love me.

I called Nikita, thinking she could still be up at four in the morning, but she was asleep—pregnant and probably cuddling with her new boy, Juan. I continued dancing in my bedroom and scribbling notes. I had a feeling I'd be embarrassed tomorrow for calling everyone, but I didn't care.

Somehow, the sun came up, and I called Candace at six in the morning. I wanted to talk to somebody—anybody—a human being. It didn't matter who it was. I was on drugs, and I knew I'd regret taking them. How did drugs become an answer to sadness? I used to deal with sadness by talking about feelings and through exercise and yoga. And now? Alcohol, jealousy, Molly, and cocaine. While on Molly, I felt absolutely normal. I was sober. Just extra loving. Was that my true self?

I loved life, and deep inside, I knew I wanted to live for as long as God (or whatever had created me) intended. I had felt safe and protected at Cookie's strip club, but I didn't respect myself then. Molly made me believe in myself and gave me the courage and confidence to dig deeper inside the young Chardonnay. I had felt confident while young, sexy, and desirable, but where was that confidence now? Why did I only have confidence while on Molly?

I lay down on the air mattress at eight in the morning, and sleep somehow, finally, kidnapped me away to dreamland.

Fifty-Seven

Growing up near Disney World, dreaming big was in my blood. A girl with nothing starts with nothing: no parents, siblings, or other support system whatsoever. Anything more than nothing is *something*. You start with little wishes, like to earn enough money to buy your first ice cream. It feels so gratifying when you accomplish something you've always dreamed of. But the excitement wears off, and you start dreaming bigger. Now to get a high, you must buy a phone. You save for months or maybe years, perhaps even stealing or murdering to get what you want. After buying more expensive items, the excitement lasts equally longer, but eventually, it wears off. What's bigger than a phone? A car, a condo, a star named after you. Your name on a movie poster. Does the ego ever stop dreaming?

Then I learned about the theory of the hedonic treadmill. Hedonists believe that the most important part of life is to pursue pleasure and happiness. For some, it could mean adventures, and for others, it could mean life-threatening situations. Thrillists are another category; they predominantly seek thrills, like jumping with a parachute. What can possibly be bigger than that? Jumping from the moon? Hedonists are a milder version of thrillists, their boring cousins, if you will.

The hedonic treadmill is our basic level of happiness, and no matter what happens, good and bad, we eventually return to some sort of normalcy, a constant level of happiness that will always be there no matter what. Happiness and grief, therefore, eventually wear off. The death of someone no longer hurts as much, and a new phone no longer feels exciting.

We run on a hedonic treadmill because that's just how life is. The problem comes when lots of positive experiences happen quickly, and your perception of happiness changes. You think your happiness actually increases. Until it all comes crumbling down from unstable cornerstones, erroneously put in place. Therefore, if I were to write a formula for happiness, I would go completely mathematical.

Happiness (*H*) is a constant, then. We always toggle between positive and negative experiences, and happiness, in a sense, could be a positive experience or a negative experience, or what we call life (L). Life happens over time (T).

$$H = L \times T$$

Eventually, the thrill of a new car or the devastation of a house foreclosure wears off, so long as, in a perfect world, no more positive or negative experiences accelerate in the interim. But who are we kidding, right? Typically, positive and negative experiences happen in packs of two or more. Therefore, if positive or negative experiences accelerate quickly, there's a spike of an emotion that your mind cannot possibly sustain for a long time. So you crash emotionally.

Unhappiness, or negative happiness ($-H$), could be summed up similarly, but whereas positive and negative experiences double, the time spent experiencing such emotions decreases:

$$-H = 2L \times T/2$$

So happiness or unhappiness, at least according to these formulas, is quite literally about acceleration. I could sum up my summer spent with Cinnamon as following a sharp curve of unhappiness. I dove into that friendship like a thrillist jumping from an airplane, excited, like a child, to reunite with the past, blinded by seemingly positive experiences. And just as rapidly, happiness vanished.

You could say happiness and unhappiness are about easy come, easy go. What you take away from an experience is what matters. We'll all eventually return to the constant happiness (H), for the negative, as seen in mathematical formulas, can be moved to the other side and be forgotten about.

Part Ten

Rikers

Embrace the glorious mess that you are.

—ELIZABETH GILBERT

Fifty-Eight

I was so blinded by the excitement I could barely breathe. I noticed Cookie before she noticed me, and the grim reality brought me back to Earth.

Ah, assumptions. I waited for the Cookie I had in my mind—crispy, tasty, and satisfying. Whoever exited, handcuffed and in an orange uniform, was an impersonator, someone whose name must have been Crumble.

She no longer had smooth, lustrous skin. Wrinkles, for the removal of which she used to pay lots of dough, had appeared with a lack of thereof. Cookie had never been a skinny woman, but now she was doughier, full of salt, sugar, and gluten. Unhappiness tends to accumulate in the middle of the stomach, rounding our waists, and with the past month alone, I no longer possessed a flat belly either. I was in ranks with Aspen, Cinnamon, and soon Cookie. Food brings comfort, and besides, who said you must be skinny to be happy? The formula for happiness does not indicate that anywhere.

Her eye possessed a shiner, a colorful prize perhaps awarded by another inmate. Cookie is of Dominican descent, and she used to wear colorful wigs, a trend most of the girls followed at the strip club. Now she had a military cut, either by choice or demand, but the effect was mystifying.

Cookie was a born dominatrix, a woman who handcuffed men for a living, providing humiliation and punishment services, and now it came around. Life goes in circles, and we call them karma. While I hated Cinnamon right then, I agreed with her that people like Cookie take advantage of young girls, and although I don't agree that anyone should be treated like an animal and sent to jail, I found her lack of freedom fitting somehow. But I was delighted I had the freedom to walk away from that place.

"Hi, Chardonnay, so good to see you," I had imagined her saying as we hugged, but it never occurred.

When Cookie recognized me, her face underwent, if not utter disgust, a definite transformation in that direction.

"What are you doing in this shithole?" was her opening.

"Aspen and Cinnamon told me you were here."

"What are you doing with the likes of those two? I thought you were actually the smart one."

"No, I'm not friends with them anymore."

"So what brings you here?"

"I just wanted to see you."

"Just wanted to see me? Bullshit. If I learned nothing from this place, I learned nothing is *just*. What do you want? You can be brief."

I remembered Cookie being stern, which was exactly what I needed at twenty-one, but now, at least according to the formula for unhappiness, her life was occurring at record speed in half the time allotted, and therefore her sternness had become bitterness.

At twenty-six, I wanted at least mentorship from her, if not love. Cookie was aging prematurely, and the way she was treated in jail, like a savage, had made her one. I didn't imagine she'd get right down to business, but I guess that's what a businesswoman does, even in jail. As her life accelerated and her time on Earth decreased, she skipped the chitchat. So I dived straight into it.

"I ran into Cinnamon at the store where she works, called Lyon's."

"I know where they work."

I stumbled for words. "Cinnamon introduced me to drugs, and now my boss wants me to be a dominatrix behind closed doors. And somehow, I ended up mixed up in that mess, and I'm struggling to get out."

She smiled for the first time, and then a laugh escaped her lips. A pity laugh that diminished me in size.

"What did you expect from a drug user?" she asked.

"I didn't expect anything. We got close again, and she tricked me into doing Molly until I started turning into a different person."

"Oh, this place is full of those different persons. You'll see."

I would see? Was she suggesting I would end up at Rikers?

"I need to get out of this somehow," I said.

"So what do you need?"

"I need your advice, Cookie."

"What advice? How not to end up in jail? Don't be stupid—that's how simple this is. Don't hang out with Aspen, Cinnamon, and the likes. What do you need? I'm asking for the last time."

Her patience, it seemed, diminished with every word. I had to tell her the truth.

"This will sound stupid, Cookie, but while on Molly, I realized I craved punishment the way my boss craves his. This young side of me hates that I make advances in life, and she lives at your strip club. I don't know what she wants."

Cookie rolled her eyes. "I just beat up a bitch for snitching, and you want me to tell you what you want in your past?"

"Words to that extent."

"You have a nerve."

"You owe this to me, Cookie. I did so much for your club."

"I don't owe anyone shit. You made a ton of money for yourself, and you were free to come and go whenever."

"I was young and didn't know any better."

"What are you talking about? You're allowed to drive a car at sixteen and drink at twenty-one. You gonna blame everyone for your misadventures? You're pathetic."

"Cinnamon said that adults should know better than to let young girls decide for themselves."

"Then go and listen to Cinnamon. I'll see you here soon." With that, she stood up and yelled, "Guard!"

And that was that.

Cookie turned and said, "If you want advice from a woman in jail, well, guess what? That's where you'll end up. My past brought me here, just like your past will bring you here. But you can change it if you make peace with her. I can't believe I'm saying this. But forgive yourself."

"How?"

"If I knew, I wouldn't be here."

Fifty-Nine

That night, I was lying on the air mattress, trash bags still scattered throughout my bedroom. In my head, I had an internal monologue. I talked to the young Chardonnay as if she were a real person.

Hi. Listen, I know it sounds crazy, and perhaps I am crazy, but I realized you and I, we want different things. But because we have to live together for the rest of our lives, we must be civil. People get along in prisons, or otherwise, Cookie beats them up. I know that my roommate Lisa, for example, pays so little rent, and

I had to forgive her. Cinnamon was incorrect. Nobody twisted my arm to make me be a stripper, and I cannot blame Cookie or Lisa or anyone. You and I have made those decisions together, and we must live with the consequences.

First of all, I love you, and second of all, I forgive you. You have done so much for me. You worked really hard. You were at that club, night after night, touched by disgusting men, while here I am in a lovely apartment, making my own choices about which men can touch me. It does not sound fair, but that is life. Life is not always fair. I am jealous of your beautiful body, which I no longer have, toned, tanned, and healthy. And you are jealous of my money, while I am jealous of your reckless optimism. But you are strong, and I would never be able to do this without you. We are one, you and I. And without you working with me, I will end up at Rikers, together with you. Now you have met Cookie. She is not the mother you thought she was. She was making money because she was running a business. You realized, all on your own, that you wanted to do something else. You saved up for me, and now I ruined it all. But I know the fighter in you—in me—will continue fighting.

Can we please start from scratch? I started taking Molly in July, trying to quiet you down. I felt lost and did not know who I was anymore. Drugs are never pure, despite what Cinnamon told me. They messed me up in a terrible way, and now we are both suffering.

If you do not forgive me, there is no way we can go on.

So . . . Do you forgive me?

I realized I hadn't forgiven my mom for abandoning me at the hospital in Florida. That realization was so sudden, I sat up, grabbed a journal, and scribbled:

Forgiveness

Could that be true? Forgiveness sounds like an easy concept, and we often ask for apologies without giving it another thought. When a person forgives us, we are then set free. But what if that person continues punishing us for the crime we'd committed by various tactics, such as verbal or physical abuse?

When Lisa apologized for snapping at me, I said I forgave her, but I lied. I held a grudge, which over time, multiplied my hate, in return, multiplying my unhappiness (–*H*). I wrote:

–H = Hate

What is hate, however? Are hatred and punishment the same thing? I had been punishing myself for everything. For being abandoned as a child, for being molested, for being touched for money. For drinking and drugs. And then it spiraled toward love. I punished myself for friendships, and I punished myself when somebody offered kindness but I didn't think I deserved it.

Scientists think of the Big Bang as follows: If the universe is expanding, it means back in time, trillions of years back, it must have been smaller. If we go back in time, second by second, we will see how all that expansive universe will come to a point in time when it's nothing. A dot. When no wrong had been done. No mistakes. No happiness and no unhappiness. And then there's the Big Bang, and you get born. You cry as you see the light. You bond with your mother. Slowly, as you grow older, your resentments multiply. And then you learn about forgiveness, and then what?

How can you turn the universe back into nothingness? I'd read enough books on the subject of forgiveness and optimism, but yet, none of them resonated enough to ring a bell. Does forgiveness happen overnight like euphoria, or does it occur with age? After all, we believe age brings wisdom. And yet, that never appears to be true in my experiences of dealing with people.

I wanted to forgive my mother, but I didn't know how. So happiness was not life multiplied by time but was simply forgiveness. Did that mean I must forgive everyone and exist under the sun like a pushover? Pretend that my sunflower seeds would one day bloom from rotten seeds? I wanted to give up.

So far, all my formulas for happiness had crumbled. I made lists of requirements, be they a healthy body, community, a vocation that matters, or love for yourself. I thought happiness was a mathematical formula of life because it appears to multiplied by time, the hedonic treadmill.

The Cornerstones of Happiness

$$H = L \times T$$

But the more I thought about happiness, the more concepts seemed to matter. Was happiness not a formula but a set of formulas? And what if tomorrow, forgiveness is no longer the answer?

While happiness can mean different things for different people, there must be a universal glue that holds us all together. My bets were all on forgiveness. That meant I had to forgive my mom, forgive Cookie, and forgive Cinnamon. I had to forgive Lisa and Lise. I had to forgive all the men who'd touched me inappropriately during my life and those who were given permission.

I couldn't fathom forgiving everyone anytime soon.

Sixty-One

Chloe returned from Italy, tired of traveling. While spending time in Italy sounded fun in practice, in reality, she was bored to death. So she returned to New York and applied to culinary school.

"You think that's your calling?" I asked.

"No, but when I work with my hands, there's magic going on in my head. I become ecstatic. I took a pasta-making class in Italy where we had to knead the dough, and it was the most liberating experience."

Chloe was excited about a new beginning, and new beginnings often bring out the innocence in us we believe we've lost.

In the meantime, the transgender Candice had secured a membership at Lucille Roberts, a women-only gym.

"I had no idea I'd be accepted!" she told me over the phone, excited like a little girl. "Like, this is the best news ever. Now I can finally focus on saving the money and toning my abs!"

No vagina talk. Just girl talk.

Nikita also had some news. Her ex, Jesus, had gone to prison for beating someone up, and Joaquin had been captured in Chile and would be brought to justice.

"I guess justice does exist, huh?" she asked.

"I dearly hope so," I said.

The most exciting part of life is not knowing the future, the mystery of it all. Humanity keeps reproducing because it's our nature, our normal state: the constant of life. I shouldn't blame my mom for things she didn't do, I realized, but thank her for things she did do: she brought me to this planet, despite hardships and who knows what else. And just like that, self-help books were right. Forgiveness starts with gratitude.

I practiced gratitude daily, hoping one day, forgiveness would follow. There's no forgiveness—and therefore, happiness—without hope and patience.

Sixty-Two

Suffice it to say, nobody from Lyon's, except Ichika, cared that I left. Nothing to report to the Internal Revenue Service or to the Department of Labor. Nothing to explain to the staff. On second thought, did I even work there, or was there a ghost in my place?

I hoped never to let girls like Cinnamon push me around anymore. However, unlike in May, I no longer had the safety net of $25,000. So I was in a bit of a pickle.

The consignment store gave me some money back for clothes I'd never even worn. At a pawn shop, a guy appraised my jewelry and gave me a good deal, enough to pay for my September rent and the exterminator; I even had a minuscule amount of money left over. Whatever I could, I returned back to stores, bringing my credit-card debt down. But now the interest had started accumulating as well.

I met Ichika after Labor Day in Flushing on her day off. The weather was in the mid-seventies; I borrowed one of Lise's scarves and a beret, and I looked French.

When we met for hot pot, I felt a strange connection to Ichika. We weren't that close, but as soon as I saw her, my body changed into the Wonder Woman pose. My spine straightened, shoulders back.

Ichika wanted to know what had happened and why I'd left Lyon's. I told her about my summer: Cinnamon had got me into drugs ... addiction. It was challenging and awkward to tell Ichika the truth. Ichika had overcome cancer, avoided drugs and drinking, and didn't rely on romantic relationships for self-esteem. I saw myself with a scarlet *A* imprinted in the middle of my forehead compared to her.

She laughed, assuring me not to hold my breath. In her prime (when in her twenties), Ichika did worse things, she told me, but failed to specify which.

"Which things?" I asked, intrigued.

"It was eighties. We like club. The rest for your imagination."

"Thanks for making me feel better."

"Sometime, Mizumi, thing happen for good reason. Cinnamon make you take drug, and now you no work with her. That good. She left after you."

"Who left?"

"Cinnamon."

"She did?"

"And Aspen follow. Lyon hire two guy right away. So young and pretty. Gay. So nice to me, customer."

"Lyon hired two gay guys? My roommate Liam would love to hear that story."

"Yes. They smart. One of them, Will, tell me why my sunflower seed no grow."

"Why?" I asked, as if I hadn't known about her roasted sunflower seeds.

"He say, sunflower need sunlight. You get, Mizumi? Sun . . . flower . . . need . . . sun . . . light. That why no grow. That why is call sunflower. You understand? But he move my plant to window. And look!"

Ichika fumbled in her purse until she found her phone. She showed me a picture of the wooden planter with green shoots coming up.

"It take two day," she said. "Sunflower seed grow fast. I so happy. I wish you work there with me."

Warmth wrapped around me like a blanket, goose-bumps rising on my arms and along my spine. Why did I feel the happiness Ichika felt?

"I wish I worked with you too," I said.

"Mizumi, you call or text. I make ramen for dinner someday. You come. OK?"

"OK."

The new worker, Will, managed to find a way to help Ichika grow sunflowers without making her feel like a failure. Instead of telling her the truth—"You're so stupid, Ichika. You can't plant roasted seeds"—he'd instead planted fresh sunflower seeds, and Ichika became happier. What's a little white lie? The thing is, it really doesn't matter. There are solutions to every problem, even the most unsolvable ones, *if* there's a will. But now I wondered who would kick Lyon in the nuts with all the girls gone.

A solution to eternal happiness is much simpler and within reach of all of us, but we don't find happiness rewarding unless we overcome a struggle. And that's abuse. We disallow ourselves to experience positive emotions because we feel unworthy and undeserving. We feel guilty when others struggle. In a sense, guilt is a tool, and we use it against ourselves, hammering ourselves for things we have and have not done.

I had abused Chardonnay (with Miso's help) for disconnecting from me because my goals had changed over the years. In return, she made me feel miserable for enjoying life and freedom. The bridge between us, thankfully, was much shorter and the river much narrower. But it would have become an ocean had I continued punishing us both. So when the misogynist messaged me and invited me for a hookup after his girlfriend left town, I said, *"Sorry, I can't see you anymore."*

"Why?"

"Personal reasons."

"But you were such a great hole."

"I see how that's what you think of me. But right now, I'm looking for a boyfriend."

"You were just a hole for me, not girlfriend material. I'm upset, but adios, fatty."

Afterward, he sent a dozen text messages in uncouth, derogatory terms, stating all the reasons why *he* deserved better, angry passages of a narcissist who, similar to Cinnamon, didn't know how to deal with rejection.

Rejection and abandonment stand side by side, and we take them personally.

My addiction to Molly occasionally sent me into overdrive of emotional pits and suicidal thoughts, but I believed my neurotransmitters would soon rewire themselves, my brain wanting to survive.

But healing takes time.

I kept on running, bringing my serotonin levels up. Then I found a job as a waitress nearby—again, mostly cash through tips. But this time, I was on the payroll, microscopic as it was. First time on the payroll. I was legit.

For some reason, it felt like I was back at the beginning of summer, before accidentally stepping into Lyon's ... Except now I didn't have a savings cushion. But I had just enough, and that would sustain me while I dealt with my demons.

But when Cinnamon messaged me at the end of September, I really didn't know how to react.

Her text: *"I'm sorry, Chardonnay. Can we talk? I'm leaving for Key West in a week and wanted to clear a few things before I go. I'll be at Randy's tonight at seven. No Aspen."*

Sixty-Three

Forgiveness doesn't mean you let people walk over you. Forgiveness includes boundaries, hard conversations, and repercussions. I didn't want to let Cinnamon think she was off the hook simply because she reached out first. Cinnamon had mentioned she despised people who apologized, so by that logic (since she apologized to me), did that mean she hated herself? I could lie and tell her I'd forgiven her, and one day that would be true, but I wanted to tell the truth from now on.

While I wanted to punish her, Cinnamon and Chardonnay were still bonded, two peas in a pod, a set of earrings. Molly creates false neurotransmitter pathways and forces you to fall in love with whomever you take it with. And I connected with Cinnamon several times, enough for a lifetime. While you're on Molly, it's like falling in love a hundred times a night. The more you take it, the more you in love you are.

I learned from self-help books that love and hate are interchangeable, and in another mathematical formula, they're equal:

$$L = H$$

The more the *L*, the more the *H*. Meaning what, exactly? Meaning if you love somebody, you may just as equally hate them, but if you don't care about them, you will feel no remorse as you set them free.

A girlfriend of mine once told me, "I love him so much, it hurts!" It's because sometimes we can't distinguish the difference between the two feelings since they're one and the same. Sometimes love feels like punishment, and other times, punishment feels like love. They correlate in an extrapolative line.

I felt equal love and hate for Cinnamon. Since the scales balanced each other out, I was confused about what the truth was. Suicidal thoughts persisted, nagging at me occasionally, and I blamed Cinnamon for allowing me to deteriorate in this ditch, all alone and scared. I needed to undo the love for her somehow, and meeting her was my way of doing so.

Sixty-Four

At Randy's, Cinnamon was perched on a barstool at our regular spot in the corner. She'd been watching the door, for when I crossed the threshold, she jumped and attempted a smile, devious and deceiving. The last time at Randy's, she wanted to kill me for even mildly suggesting she was a fake friend. As always, Randy's was quiet, with only a few patrons. The air inside the bar smelled like beer because time after time, the wooden floors soaked up spilled liquids, along with dust and mud. When you keep damaging something repeatedly, the damage will become permanent. Like my brain on Molly, it seemed.

Cinnamon had recently done her lips, hair, and nails. Every girl knows that spending money is therapeutic. Her dilated pupils, however, suggested drug abuse, proved by her clenched jaw. The way Cookie put it, what should one expect from a drug user?

"Chardonnay, I'm so glad you're here, girl."

I was channeling Cookie for some reason, incapable of tolerating the chitchat.

"What do you want?" I asked abruptly.

"I wanna apologize and say goodbye. Is that OK?"

I sat down on a stool next to her, and the bartender approached me.

"Nothing for me, thanks," I told him.

He nodded in agreement, but Cinnamon interjected, "Get her a drink."

"I said no."

"You're at a bar, Chardonnay. What else will you drink here?"

"I didn't come here to drink. If you wanna apologize and say goodbye, I'm all ears."

"Chardonnay, don't be rude. Why are you rushing me?"

"Because I have better things to do."

"Why are you so infuriated? I quit Lyon's, and so did Aspen."

"Ichika told me."

"That shrew always sticks her nose in everyone's business."

"Cinnamon, if you came here to talk shit about everyone, I'm leaving."

"Relax. I'm entitled to my opinion of people. Don't be so controlling, Chardonnay."

"Your opinion of people is outdated and borderline racist."

"Cut it out, OK? You don't know half the story, Chardonnay. Did I ever tell you I slept with Lyon?"

"And?" I asked, as if it were old news.

"Lyon has an elaborate way about his business, and I've been helping him all along—for money."

"How?"

"I was hoarding cash for my escape to Key West, and I've earned enough. I wanna escape the sinking ship. And I'll tell you everything about it. But first, I used to hire girls for Lyon to enjoy. I told him not to touch you, but before you, there were numerous girls, young and naive. I'm basically Cookie, Chardonnay, and I'm so embarrassed by myself."

"That's neither here nor there, Cinnamon."

"You only see what you wanna see. Which is that I hurt you and made you take Molly. And that's why I'm sorry. I overreacted because you pointed that out. But then you showed me what a shitty person I was, and I lost it. Nobody wants to hear criticisms. I went straight to Lyon and told him he could go and fuck himself."

"So what?"

"He's been laundering cash through his business for years, and it's bound to collapse once the credit reaches its limit. He's scheming the system."

"How?"

"Once he hits his credit limit, he's filing for bankruptcy. We're talking millions of dollars of cash, Chardonnay. With that, he retires on Long Island or wherever—and none the wiser. The money is clean and untraceable, put away in cash and precious stones and invested in other legit businesses."

"Why would he go into bankruptcy with all that cash?"

"Because he's clever. He'd set up shell companies that 'make the furniture,' but in reality, he's doing a drug-dealing operation, and Lyon's is just a front. He even has investors in his stupid business, and he's scamming everyone. His creditors believe his financial records are correct. Everything looks good on the books. They gave him another million recently, and Lyon cleverly pays himself while inflating the prices on his own furniture. It's not easy to explain, dim, and shady. In the end, he sells the cheap furniture, pays 'some' taxes, and receives a commission—all in cash. It's money laundering one-oh-one."

"So what, you're going to call the police?"

"Don't you get it, Chardonnay? Lyon and Cookie both operated money-laundering businesses all along. Only Cookie got caught. And you and I have contributed half a decade to them. Doesn't that make you angry?"

"I don't wanna get angry at myself when I was twenty-one or blame Cookie and Lyon for my choices."

Cinnamon rubbed her eyes and groaned. "You were used as a device for cheating and deceit, and you're OK with that?"

"I knew what I did. I tried to survive and work. I'm not a conspiracy theorist. I just wanted some food on my plate."

"Do you even know how I met Lyon?"

"You told me you applied for a job at the store."

"That was a lie, Chardonnay. I met him at a strip club in Manhattan two years ago. One day, I walked into Lyon's furniture store, shopping for a bed just like you, and there he was, the owner of the store, who, weeks prior, begged me to kick his balls with my heels. So he then asked me to come and work for him at the store."

"And you kept it a secret from me. Why?"

"He asked me to keep it hush. Listen, he loves nasty stuff being done to him, and I was the only person who knew that at the time. He tried to keep his enemy close."

"What kind of dirty stuff?"

"Handcuffs, whips, all kinds of dominatrix stuff. He's embarrassed by it, obviously. When it comes to dirty sex, people build a facade around them. Can you imagine if it's uncovered that a macho man like Lyon is a sissy boy behind closed doors?"

"I understand now."

"You should have seen his face the day he saw me at his store in broad daylight. His whole demeanor changed, and he was pale in seconds. Listen, when people are scared, they'll do anything. He probably thought I would blab all over town that he's a submissive sissy boy in bed. Which, in retrospect, I should have. But what good would it do? A stripper blabbing shit about a businessman? Who would believe me? Besides, you don't want to mess around with criminals like Lyon and Cookie. They both have guns and connections to the mafia. Why do you think that is?"

"For protection."

"Yeah, fat chance, Chardonnay. Wake up and smell the kinky boots kicking his balls. When Lyon saw me at his store that first time, he was surprised. Guess what he did? He roofied and raped me, which he filmed on his phone. How's that for blackmail?"

"Why did you stay working for him after that?"

"Stockholm syndrome. I was falling for him because of drugs, which he hooked me on. It makes you fall in love with people for all the wrong reasons. He offered me a better life than working as a stripper, and I blindly fell for it. His plan was to launder as much money as he could before the bankruptcy."

"I don't believe you."

"At the time, I didn't understand the nuances of his money-laundering business."

"What about Ichika? Is she in the loop?"

"No. She's his wife's sister. The job gives her something to do, but she doesn't know anything. She just thinks Lyon hires pretty girls to run his business, while in reality, he hires people he can sexually abuse. It's probably better Ichika doesn't know anything. The less you know, the better you sleep. That's my mantra."

"Why are you telling me all this? I don't work there, and I don't care about Lyon or that you're leaving."

"I really wish I were stupid and naive sometimes. But I'm smart enough to understand how this world works—full of cruelty and pain. When there's nothing I can do, I hide here in the corner at Randy's and pretend life isn't so bad. I'm not a phycologist, but I'm positive Lyon gets kicked in the balls because he feels bad for scamming his creditors. At least there's *some* conscience in that cocksucker. We can do nothing at this point except try to cope with this information any way we can. Nobody is ever thrilled on this planet. Happiness is like a mirage in the desert. You reach it, and then it slips further away, leaving you tired, dehydrated, on the verge of death."

"Just like Molly," I said.

"Textbook self-punishment. Did you know that we believe suffering improves our character? We believe that physical and mental pain can restore our honesty and moral excellence. Why do we do that to ourselves, Chardonnay?" she said, shaking her head.

For the first time, Cinnamon asked a question that wasn't mean as a rhetorical one.

Sixty-Five

While watching the local news on a cold October morning, I saw Lyon on TV.

The commentator said, "Local business owner arrested on money-laundering charges. If he's convicted, he'll spend the rest of his life in prison."

I stopped listening then and texted Cinnamon right away. *"You won't believe what just happened. Lyon got arrested!"*

She was typing:

. . .

. . .

Then she erased what she'd written and started typing again.

. . .

. . .

It was going to be a long message, I thought. But when my phone pinged, her message had only two words and a smiling emoji at the end: "*You're welcome.*"

Sixty-Six

Suffice it to say, the news caught Ichika by surprise and, even more so, Lyon's wife, whose reality had become a total nightmare—public scrutiny and loathing.

As for me, that week had been particularly hard from a happiness standpoint. Some days were better than others. My brain craved an abundance of neurotransmitters. I was so depressed, I had no idea what to do. Then the news about Lyon came, and it simply overwhelmed me.

What did "You're welcome" refer to? Was Cinnamon involved somehow? Maybe she felt bad about the whole situation and somehow got involved. Untraceable, as she'd never been on the books. A whistleblower.

Happiness . . .

The more I read about happiness, however, the less happy I proportionally became. Yes, forgiveness, a sense of belonging, and friendships help. A funny movie helps. You can be happy with drugs or without them. But when your world crumbles, what do you do? What holds us together? There must be something inside us that literally holds us together like cells, our building blocks.

I found out something incredibly interesting that day. There are proteins inside our cells called *kinesins* that walk along microtubules, carrying cargo such as neurotransmitters to our brains' neurons. Something inside our cells with two legs walks around carrying happiness. Each step requires energy. A kinesin delivers a neurotransmitter where it needs to be, jumps off the microtubule, swims back to the beginning, and jumps back on to carry more—just a simple constant of life—over and over and over again.

Life is a constant supply of wonders, happy moments, or grim surprises. But if these small proteins can keep us together and work tirelessly to supply happiness, why not get up and just try?

Epilogue

Sanity and happiness are an impossible combination.

— MARK TWAIN

Memories weaken with time, the effects of drugs wear off, and what are we left with after all is said and done? What is our purpose on Earth? Are we ever pleased?

I craved to have a mom my entire life because that word—*mom*—connotates happiness in my mind. And because I'd never had a mom, I sought one anywhere I went, trying to obtain the unattainable, proving to myself that happiness is a formula and proving myself wrong. I found a "mom" in Lisa and Lise, Ichika and Cinnamon, and even Nikita and Candace. My mom had never been a physical person, but bits of her had been found in everyone.

Life proceeds whether we like it or not. In real time. The Earth will orbit the sun, and the moon will change its shape twelve times per year.

Happiness and unhappiness are two feelings akin to two vectors on a graph, and they change their trajectory based on circumstances. All you have to do is change their velocity and, consequently, their trajectories. Something good or bad happens, one vector shoots up, and the other shoots down. Over and over and over again.

Just life, in real time . . .

After moving to Key West, Aspen and Cinnamon found a job at a bar right on the beach (together, of course)—the way Cinnamon desired. Cinnamon hated Cookie because they were similar, and I hated Cinnamon for a while because . . . we were identical as well. Love and hate are one and the same, and I realized we will always seek similarity in love and friendships.

Lisa, Lise, and Liam did the same things they'd always done. Lisa's juicer ran nonstop, Lise's boots were all over the place, and Pisces Liam cried while watching movies. One night, Lisa and Lise told me why they're so frugal. Like Aspen and Cinnamon, they're already saving for their retirement. I guess they weren't that different from Aspen and Cinnamon after all.

Chloe, Candace, and Nikita lived their lives as usual too. Chloe enjoyed her culinary school, but she felt exhausted, and I gathered she'd complain even if she became a billionaire; that's just who Chloe is.

Candace loved her gym for women, yet something was missing. Oh, her vagina . . . So we were back to that.

And Nikita kept posting positive affirmations, but this time, I realized the affirmations weren't meant for us. They were meant for her.

So standard stuff . . . life.

Lyon would be put away for life, but Cookie would be out by January, in a few months. Ichika would retire sometime—but her new job had become helping her sister overcome the horrendous public crisis caused by Lyon. Be the touchstone for her. Lyon's wife's world had flipped upside down, and who knows what could save her.

The most important thing is, we are all alive, and there are proteins in our cells that'll keep walking as long as we want them to.

But humans plant roasted seeds occasionally and make mistakes. One day, things will change for us, or maybe they won't—that's the beauty of it—the mystery of life.

But my life is my constant, the life I've chosen. It is simple yet challenging in many ways, and that life is all I have because it is mine. I am imperfect on many levels, but I realize imperfections mean I am normal. I'm upset when things go wrong, and I'm moody when clouds cover the sun. But when sunshine eventually returns, life resumes.

Nobody's perfect. I've learned that trying to achieve happiness is just like trying to achieve anything else in life. When the happiness of buying your first ice cream wears off, you go for something more significant because you no longer feel that high. That model suggests a never-ending search for happiness, the so-called "hedonic treadmill."

We are wired to compete with each other, and if there's nobody else around, we enter a contest with ourselves: with ourselves in the past. Because humans must compete. As the years progress, we may achieve dreams that satisfy us in a particular moment, but that only makes the person inside us—the one from years earlier who wished them in the first place—jealous. It's unfair to "them" that we achieved "their" dreams when they worked hard for "their" goals. Weird, huh? This circle of life is so habitual for us that we don't realize we punish, diminish, and sabotage ourselves. We're in a contest with our younger selves, a million of which can emerge in a given lifetime. A fifteen-year-old in me can scream in agony about the fact that at twenty-six, I have my own bedroom, and she'll try hurting me—for one simple reason: that she doesn't have it and I do. And those voices inside our minds telling us how horrible we are could be the inner judge who wants to be heard. That's the inner child who's struggling and who wants to be hugged.

Meditation is a practice of quieting these voices down, and meditation can bring inner peace. The more you let your inner saboteur talk, the more involved it gets in your life.

During my depersonalization caused by Molly, I saw two Lindsays fighting for the spotlight. But until I realized it wasn't a contest, I couldn't find peace inside me . . .

Happiness is a constant, and we ultimately return to it. Eventually, ripples at sea calm down. Audio waves diminish the longer they travel. And ups and downs will lessen similarly. Trying to find a universal formula for a concept of happiness is like trying to get a quick fix with a drug. The higher the high, the harder the fall. And boy did I learn that the hard way.

Acknowledgment

The author would like to express gratitude to the following people: Andrea. I miss you and I'm happy that I've met you. Mary and Bibi, COVID-19 brought us together in the most unexpected way—and I'm grateful for that. And Andres, my lockdown partner, thank you for your patience and wisdom. I would like to thank Kristen, my editor, who gave my novel a great makeover. What insights! Thank you Jerry for the interior work and Tanja for the beautiful cover. It is truly artistic!

About the Author

Jeremy Taylor was born in the USSR on August 21, 1987. He grew up in the heart of Siberia, near Lake Baikal, in a town remote and distant, buried under a frosty white blanket nine months out of the year. During the winter, Siberia remained at a constant standstill. There was nothing to do but read books and drink hot tea while ferocious winds endlessly howled and while blizzards left snowflake patterns on the windows.

Obsessed with books, Jeremy wrote his first story at age nine and has not stopped since. He is grateful for his poor and underprivileged background because he believes it helped him dream, hope, and believe. At 19, with $100 from his grandma, Jeremy ended up in Washington D.C. as a live-in au pair for a year—and then fate took over.

His favorite authors are Sue Grafton, Elizabeth Gilbert, Brené Brown, Tosha Silver, Joan Rivers, Judy Blume, Chelsea Handler, Jacqueline Susann, Don Miguel Ruiz, Haruki Murakami, Eleanor Brown, Lawrence Block, James Dashner, Lori Gottlieb, Paulo Coelho.

www.ingramcontent.com/pod-product-compliance
Lightning Source LLC
Chambersburg PA
CBHW020559310726
48979CB00008B/1278/J

* 9 7 8 1 7 3 6 1 2 7 7 3 5 *